A story of love, deceit and treachery in the magical world

THE LEPRECHAUN AND ME

SHARA LOBO

BLUEROSE PUBLISHERS
India | U.K.

Copyright © Shara Lobo 2024

All rights reserved by author. No part of this publication may be reproduced, stored in a retrieval system or transmitted in any form or by any means, electronic, mechanical, photocopying, recording or otherwise, without the prior permission of the author. Although every precaution has been taken to verify the accuracy of the information contained herein, the publisher assumes no responsibility for any errors or omissions. No liability is assumed for damages that may result from the use of information contained within.

BlueRose Publishers takes no responsibility for any damages, losses, or liabilities that may arise from the use or misuse of the information, products, or services provided in this publication.

For permissions requests or inquiries regarding this publication, please contact:

BLUEROSE PUBLISHERS
www.BlueRoseONE.com
info@bluerosepublishers.com
+91 8882 898 898
+4407342408967

ISBN: 978-93-6261-592-3

Cover design: Sadhna Kumari
Typesetting: Pooja Sharma

First Edition: July 2024

I thank God Almighty that this book could finally see the light of the day. I thank my parents Mr. John Francis Lobo and Mrs. Celine Lobo for their prayers and good wishes. I want to thank my husband, Dr. Sandeep Kumar Ram who supported me.

I dedicate this book to my children Anaya, Ayana, and Aanya, who taught me the art of storytelling, a ritual I follow before I put them to sleep every night.

Contents

Chapter 1: The Sweet Beginnings 1
Chapter 2: The Bad Omen 6
Chapter 3: Christmas Eve 11
Chapter 4: Shocking Lunch 16
Chapter 5: Disaster Ahead 21
Chapter 6: Goodbyes 26
Chapter 7: The Reunion 31
Chapter 8: Family Meeting 37
Chapter 9: Welcome Party 42
Chapter 10: Business Lunch 47
Chapter 11: The Hospital Visit 52
Chapter 12: Work, Work, and More Work 56
Chapter 13: The First Kiss 62
Chapter 14: Missing 68
Chapter 15: Uninvited 74
Chapter 16: The Bond 80
Chapter 17: Home at Last 87
Chapter 18: Midnight Truths 92
Chapter 19: Deliverance 101
Chapter 20: Wedding Bells 111
Chapter 21: Change of Plans 117
Chapter 22: Visit to the Dungeon 124

Chapter 23: New Acquaintances 132
Chapter 24: Freed at Last 137
Chapter 25: Love Conquers 149

Chapter 1

The Sweet Beginnings

Usually, Christmas is an annual festival celebrating the birth of Jesus Christ. Around Christmas, all vendors are busy exhibiting their ornaments and giftable, shops are lit with lights and wreaths made of holly. Every corner has a lot to say. People love the hustle and bustle of the holiday season as it is a time to make merry and prepare for the coming of Jesus the Savior, the king of peace, love, and joy. People were busy looking at the latest displays, choosing presents, and trying on new clothes, and children were busy eating candies, and pastries, and choosing clothes and decorations with their parents. Christmas trees were to be bought along with all types of decorations. Many people are in town to meet their family and acquaintances; they shop around the market's alleys and join in to pay for food & drinks because everybody wants to relax, make merry, and show how happy they are. The climate was perfect, the cold breeze with an orange sky as the sun set, everyone knew it would get dark soon as the night approached.

"Have we got everything on the list, Papa?" Clove asked her father. Clove was a calm, intelligent girl; pale-skinned with an angular face and red curly hair that she loved letting loose. The freckles on her face made her even more lovable; her expressive green eyes looked up to meet her father's, for a favorable answer. "Almost done dear, Well! Are you hungry? Can I get you a little something to eat? I do have to pick some things from the bakers, if that is fine with you or should I drop you home first and come back later?" Charles looked at Clove hoping for an affirmative reply. Charles was a tailor by profession, excellent in his job, resulting in the elite, rich, and famous favoring him. He would tend to people from all levels of society; was kind to people and always helped the needy. During Christmas, he stitched clothes for poor children with leftover material. Charles was tall, lean, pinkish, and well-groomed with thick black hair. His black eyes and cheeks with dimples made women's hearts flutter, his heart only yearned for Chloe; his wife and the mother of his daughter. This Christmas season was amazing, Charles got the majority of the orders finished just in time and why wouldn't he? He had stitched a new suit for the mayor who didn't stop bragging about how well he loved the fit. After that, the orders flowed, keeping him day in and out, yet he was free at last to go shopping. Who wouldn't? It was Christmas! Including the fact that he promised Clove shopping and he was a man of his word.

"Will we be going to Sweet Tooth, Daddy? I wonder what is new on display. Uncle Connor has not been home for a while. He always brings me stuff Aunt Camila bakes. Oh! I miss those ginger cookies." Clove sounded excited. "Hold your horses, young lady, yes we are headed there. Let us pick up something to surprise mummy, what do you say?" Charles responded. The next thing they knew, both their feet subconsciously headed towards the shop they were familiar with. As they walked past the shops they could hear Christmas carols. Clove hummed along with them till she reached Uncle Connor's shop. Clove swung open the door, and the sound of the wind chimes caught Uncle Connor's attention. Uncle Connor was lean and tall. He had blond hair and when he smiled; his black eyes lit, his smile was the cherry on the cake. "Finally, you folks made it. I was beginning to worry about my favorite little customer! Camila was already missing you." Connor spoke as he greeted Clove with a peck on the cheek and gave a warm hug to Charles.

Charles, Chloe, Connor, and Camila all went to school and college together making them the best of friends. Later, Cupid struck them. Connor and Camila were indeed a fun-loving couple. Camila always wanted to bake, and be an entrepreneur while Connor was alright about hanging in there for her. He was happy to help in what made her happy. They had lost their unborn child and Camila's uterus was abnormal to have another; doctors had proposed adoption but Camila wanted her baking as a distraction, they dearly clung to Clove as she was indeed the joy in their lives. Clove was lucky she had loving parents and Uncle Connor& Aunt Camila to spoil her.

Connor called Camila to meet Clove; her response was quick, "Yes! Coming dear!" Aunt Camila was slim and beautiful, she too had red curly hair always tied in a bun, and she was fair with freckles just like Clove. She brought two decorated boxes, one she handed to Charles and the other to Clove. Aunt Camila exclaimed, "Merry Christmas! I am Santa today." She winked at Charles who opened his box to find a Christmas Candle along with homemade Jam. Meanwhile, Clove was already munching on her ginger cookies, Camila knew her likings well. As the adults caught up on each other; Clove strayed away to see the display, there was the Plum Cake, Apple Cake, Christmas Chocolate Yule Log, Orange scone wedges, Apple pie, Bread & Butter pudding, Mozzarella& Tomato Tarts, White Chocolate Cheesecake Tarts and so on, the list was endless.

Clove turned towards them slowly walking. Connor had kept them busy in conversation. "I think we all need a break from the business, the cleaning, cooking, and preparing so I booked us all tickets to the Pantomime – *Robin Hood and his Merry Men*. One of the merry men was my customer, he was boasting about the show to his friends. I thought to myself why don't I walk up to him and ask for a booking? But, it turned out that the gentleman was kind enough to give me 5 passes to the event. It's at 8:00 pm. You either turn up for it or get ready for your ass to be kicked." Connor jokingly threatened Charles. Charles heartily accepted the offer, promising to check with Chole to let them know. "What's a Pantomime?" Clove questioned eagerly. "Oh! Dear me! I guess you haven't been to one yet. It's when you tell the audience a story where the performers express themselves through gestures without speaking while the music is played as an accompaniment." Camilla responded. "It is mostly slapstick comedy. I guess, you will love it. Let us work a deal, we will pick you up if your parents can't make it. Would you love that?" Connor pitched. "Yes! I would," Clove responded. This wasn't the first time that she would be out with them, she was very well cared for and enjoyed all the love and attention they both showered. She was indeed fascinated by how a story can be told without words. Clove and Charles wished them goodbye returning to the car to head home. If they were planning to go for the Pantomime, then they would have to hurry. It was 6 pm; the sun was set. The cold breeze was making Clove's ears and nose tip numb but now Clove was excited, hoping to enjoy what lay before her. In 20 minutes, they reached home, ringing the doorbell. Mom was prompt to answer. Chole was all tired from cleaning, setting up the home, and cooking; all she wanted was to raise her feet on a cushion as her feet were swollen and hurt. She wanted to watch some late-night show on the television with a cold glass of wine. Charles called up Connor and asked him to pick up Clove. It was a matter of time before the doorbell rang and Clove was all set to go. She quickly freshened up, putting on her jeans and an oversized pullover sweater but Chloe put on all warm clothing; Clove could tell from the view in the mirror that she was better dressed than the stuffed turkey.

In no time, she was out on the driveway in the car with Camila and Connor. Chole decided to sit by the fire, hearing music while Charles decided to make her meatballs and spaghetti as that was all he could make along with Christmas pudding. He wanted her to rest as this was a busy week for both of them; it was his time to show her how much importance she held for him.

Chapter 2

The Bad Omen

"Would you like me to fill the bathtub with warm water for you to relax in, Madam? A glass of fine wine along with a three-course meal with whatever little I can do; shall I say we meet in 45 minutes dressed in our pajamas and all set for our dinner date?" Charles had a twinkle in his eyes as he spoke. "Are you sure? I would love that! Just don't burn down the kitchen we just got the whitewashing done." Chole replied jokingly. Charles handed her a glass of chilled wine as Chloe headed up the stairs happy, on her way to the bathroom.

Charles worked his way into the kitchen like a seasoned chef with all the burners in full swing. He was cooking chicken soup as he found readymade soup packets; frying chicken nuggets, cutting the cheese cubes, making green salads, boiling spaghetti, putting ingredients for the sauce together, and leaving the meat marinating at the kitchen counter. All the while, his thoughts racing through his mind were 'cooking takes a lot of action in the kitchen.' He would prefer stitching, thanking his stars that he was not a chef yet despite all the hardships he would love to cook for the woman who mattered in his life.

"Do we have something on the plate, yet I am starving! The bath did me good. Thank you." Commented Chloe. She threw her arms around her loving husband, embracing him from behind. The warm hug brought a smile to their faces. They didn't want to break free.

Charles was the first to speak, "Darling, I think you will be quite impressed with me with the show I will put on. I think you will agree that I am getting better at my cooking skills every passing year." "Well, I guess I'll let the food do the talking for I am afraid it would be all hype and the fizz should frizzle down before we know," Chloe replied with a smile on her face.

Charles dimmed the dining room lights, decorated the table with a tablecloth placed two flower vases in the center, he placed lit candles; which were on the candle bar in the center between the flower vases. He played soft music drawing a chair for his lady to be seated on. She sat down in the chair, following the lead. She had planned an evening to rest so, this came as a surprise to her. Charles went into the kitchen coming out with a bowl of hot, piping chicken soup. Chloe was impressed giving him a peck on the cheek. Charles and Chloe were taken back in time to when they were in college, the love was in the air, remembering their college canteen lunch breaks. It has been 13 years since yet, it still felt like yesterday. Charles kept on bringing the courses; there was more laughter, wine, and eventually a dance.

Clove sat between Conner and Camilla. The lights were on while the audience found their seats in the middle. Luckily, their seats were in the middle of the balcony. It was amazing to know Connor knew most of the elite there. Nevertheless, many came up to them to place their orders for the Christmas season. It was time for the show to begin, and the lights were dimmed. The play was introduced warning that this was not for the faint-hearted, you could choose to leave. It was an interactive pantomime but the timely music and comic made them sit through it. The theatre was roaring with laughter, why wouldn't it? The performers were skilled. Two hours passed, and there were hot dogs, sandwiches, and soda. Clove, Camilla, and Conner were full. When the show ended they went to the green room to get autographs from all the artists. It was time to go home. The trio were tired needing a good sleep. The ride back was noisier as Clove kept talking about the parts that she loved the best. In return, Conner and Camila shared their various theatrical experiences, Conner laughed and said, "You know darling, if I wouldn't be a cashier I'd been an artist." To which both girls unanimously exclaimed that they loved the cashier better.

As they approached the home, they could see Charles and Chloe dancing through the window. They looked happy and the dim lights made them look so much in love. The three tip-toed out of the car trying their very best to not be seen. The love birds were oblivious to the three musketeers approaching through the backyard, in a matter of minutes Connor burst and opened the door all rushing in when they reached the drawing-room yelling in unison, "Surprise!" Charles and Chloe were pleasantly taken aback as they were so engrossed with each other that they didn't sense their presence.

All settled down while Clove went upstairs to change. Conner was proudly showing off the autographs he had while imitating Robin Hood. They filled them in on the best parts and time and repeatedly stated that they missed them. Chloe brought them hot coffee everyone was pleased to have it.

"Chloe, you have forgotten to put a lit candle by the window pane," Camila exclaimed, surprised. "Why do we have to do that Aunty?" questioned Clove, who had changed into her night pajamas. "It has been a tradition for as long as I can remember; my mom did it too. I guess it's a way we welcome Mary and Joseph into our house as they didn't find a place back then," Camila responded.

"Dad and I did buy candles," added Clove. "Yes, honey we were waiting for you. We thought we would light it together," Chloe said warmly, moving her hand over her daughter's head. "Ok! Let's do it now," Charles announced, excited. He brought five new candles; one by one they lit them all as they stood by the French window each looking at their candles, the light shining brightly.

It was now late and they all had a busy day. They called it a night; The trio went to see off Camila and Connor who promised to come over to attend Christmas Mass together. Clove was the first one to enter, she rushed to the window and exclaimed, "Oh dear me! Dad's candle is off!" Chloe rushed to see for herself what her daughter had just said, her heart fluttered, and she was anxious. 'A bad omen' she thought to herself, 'I hope nothing should happen to Charles.' She was dependent on him. Above all, it has been so long together and life without each other would be impossible.

Charles sensed her concern and lovingly patted her shoulder calmly saying, "Sweetheart, I am going to be here for a long time. Nothing, not even God cannot take me away from you. I have a long way to go and along with that, some splendid work to do." Chloe had tears in her eyes but in her heart, she knew that people claimed that the Titanic would never sink, but it did on its maiden voyage. All she knew was that Charles was a good man and God would never let her down. Charles lit the candle once again, and all went upstairs. They tucked Clove in bed, kissing her good night.

They went to their room changing into their night dress. Both lay in the bed. They were hugging each other eagerly waiting for Christmas Eve. Both of them knew they had a big day ahead; they had to get ready for Midnight Mass and they were excited about opening the

Christmas presents they had brought for each other. Santa was coming, Clove had to be prepared to welcome him and Rudolph. Although, Clove tried very hard she could not be up to meet them every year. This time it was different as she was determined to do so.

Chapter 3

Christmas Eve

Clove came downstairs to see her parents packing Christmas sweets for the neighbors. It was a family tradition that that passed down from her ancestors. Charles's grandfather had migrated and settled into the town and it is usually this time of the year when you miss your family the most. As a goodwill gesture, they used to share the Christmas joy with the neighbors, and since then, it has been a tradition they always cherished. In return, they got love, appreciation, and timely help, which gave them a sense of belongingness.

Clove quickly had her breakfast and joined them. It took all morning for them to finish packing but at the end of it, they were hungry again. They sat around the dining table having lunch while Charles happily mentioned some old memories about his childhood and the Christmas he spent with his family. Chloe also would remember the fun she had with her siblings. However, they had not been in touch with anyone. Chloe missed them. They lived in the city as well as the fact that Chloe's family didn't approve of Charles since he was not from an affluent family and merely thought low of Charles back then. Charles was jobless and studying but today, it was different he had made a name for himself. He had everything that her father would have wanted his daughter to have, it's been so long and he wanted them to communicate with her even if they did not accept him.

The clock struck 2:00 pm alerting Chloe. "Charles, we need to iron our clothes and lay down everything in place or else we will be late for midnight mass," an anxious Chloe blurted out her fears. Chloe began to clear the dishes while Charles and Clove started working on the ironing. It took them an hour, but they were all set by 3 pm. All the dresses were stiffly ironed, shoes polished, matching jewelry and accessories were laid out and when all was good they went upstairs to rest.

Connor and Camila were there as promised. It was 7 pm and this time dinner was on them. Camila made Apple Tarts, Potato soup, Shepherd's Pie, Chicken stew, and Bread pudding. Chole was quick to make coffee for everyone. After dinner was served, all had eaten to their heart's content they went to their respective rooms to change. Whenever it was late Connor and Camila stayed back in the guest room.

Charles wore a dark navy blue-colored suit with a sky-colored shirt to match. Conner wore a dark green-colored suit with a light green-color shirt. Camila wore a grey-colored suit with a white lacy shirt. Chloe wore a short red A-line dress with a string of pearls and Clove wore a purple-colored frock with a matching bow to go with it. All were set to attend the Midnight mass.

Connor, Camila, and Clove went to church ahead to catch place for, it would be jam-packed tonight meanwhile, Charles and Chloe left the gifts at the bottom of the tree. Connor and Camila had placed their gifts on their way out. Chloe placed a glass of warm milk with cookies for Santa and a carrot for Rudolph. Charles and Chloe locked the door and were on the road to catch up with them.

The Church was lit and there was a huge crib made. Everyone who had come was greeting one another, some were clicking pictures. As they approached; the choir was singing Christmas carols Chloe said, "Charles we made it to church on time as usual. Look Aunt Pamela beat us; she is seated at the front row wearing a black evening gown." Charles quickly scanned for Clove and asked Chloe to follow him. They were reunited and sat together for the mass as Camila had kept a place for them. The altar was decorated with roses, and the candles lit. On one side a tall Christmas tree was placed and decorated.

The pews were decorated with red bows, the red carpet was placed in the middle. The choir sang the entrance hymn and all arose, the mass was solemn but all along what raced in Clove's mind was she did not want to miss Santa and his presents. She wanted to touch Rudolph the reindeer. This time she wanted to catch him unlike always.

It was past midnight; in the wee hours, they returned home as the mass took time, and by the time they left wishing everyone 'Merry Christmas,' it was indeed late. Reverend Father Tony prayed over Clove and other children, the sick, and the elderly.

Upon entering home, Clove raced everyone to the Christmas tree finding that Santa had already drank the milk & ate the cookies. Rudolph had nibbled on the carrot. This time they had arrived early who could blame them they were busy; all the children were waiting for their presents. "Well! Dear, better luck next time," assured Camila. "Let's open our presents!" said Connor excited while saying that he had already reached his stockings. Connor was acting like a child and his eyes were all shining to know what he had gotten. Camila had brought him a red sweater, Chloe gifted him a solar calculator which was new in the market, Charles had gifted him a nice watch and Clove had gifted him a box of chocolates. On the other hand, Camila got a lovely top from Chloe, Charles gifted her a watch, Connor brought her a charms gold bracelet and Clove gifted her perfume. Charles was excited to open his presents, Chloe had gifted him a new pair of shoes, Connor gifted him a diary with a pen, Camila gifted him a grey shirt and Clove got a green tie for him. Chloe was shy but relented to the peer pressure to open the presents, Camila had gifted her a black dress, Connor had gifted her perfume, Charles had gifted her gold earrings which were floral in design, and lastly, Clove got her red lipstick. Finally, Clove opened her presents, Camila gifted her 'Pride and Prejudice' a novel by Jane Austen, Connor gifted her jewelry, Charles gave her colors to paint, and Chloe got her a T-shirt that said: '*I Rock*!'. Above all, Santa gifted her a walkie-talkie talkie which she could play with her friends. "I have to thank Santa," Clove exclaimed, grateful. "Maybe Uncle Connor can help you post a card thanking him or if he has friends, they could deliver it to him by hand. What do you say, darling, could that be arranged?" Camila pitched in so that Clove could get a sense of satisfaction. "I think I could do that. Anything for my lady. Your wish is my command," Conner responded, smiling.

All of them were laughing at what Conner said. Camila was all shy, blushing; the deep red color of the blush on her cheek was visible.

"It is late, let us call it a night. Tomorrow is a big day. We are going to have a great meal from my world-renowned chef. Let us give her a good night's sleep, why don't you stay back?" Requested Charles. "I do not feel so. We will head back as the bakery has to be opened tomorrow but we will keep it open for half a day only. Let us go, Camila," replied Connor as he and Camila arose.

"Well, we had a wonderful time. See you tomorrow for lunch," Charles said as he closed the door while Connor and Camila both headed towards the car to get back home.

Chapter 4

Shocking Lunch

The next day, Clove woke up to the Christmas carols played by her father. Clove was excited about today's lunch as Connor and Camila would be there, she wondered what Camila would bring her this time. She just loved Camila's sweet treats.

Clove brushed her teeth, freshened up, took a bath, and dressed up. She loved the frills in her dress, the green color looked great and the green bow matched her dress. 'Papa knows best.' This is what rang in her mind. He had carefully chosen the fabric for her and stitched a bow with the leftover material. Clove quickly headed downstairs to meet her mother and father sitting at the dining table having their breakfast. "Ah! There you are we were wondering what took you so long!" Charles said grinning as Clove came over to hug him. "Oh! My darling you look so beautiful! Charles, indeed you have done a good job once again," exclaimed Chloe. "Thank you, darling," Charles responded. There was bread, fried eggs, bacon, sausages, fried tomatoes & mushrooms, a glass of warm milk, orange juice, and the cookie goodies that Camilla had given Clove earlier. Clove along with her parents finished her breakfast quickly with Charles helping her in clearing & washing the dishes while Chole started working on the lunch menu. Charles and Clove had decided to share the Christmas goodies & cakes with the neighbors while Chloe was working on the Christmas lunch which included lamb roast, roasted potatoes &

veggies, stuffed goose, and Christmas pudding added to the fact that Camilla would bring a fine bottle of wine with traditional Irish cake and buttered fried scallops. Chloe worked in the kitchen, she liked it when it was quiet and calm as she was anxious; cooking wasn't her cup of tea like Camila but yes, if she was determined she could put one of the best dishes on the table.

It was one o'clock, and Connor and Camila would be home anytime soon. The table was set yet, Chloe anxiously paced the living room till the doorbell rang. Chloe was quick to answer the doorbell and to her surprise, it was Charles and Clove. Both were back from their Christmas sharing errand in return, they had got a fine bottle of wine from Ryan, the Christmas cake from Drake, and Christmas cookies from Aunt Pamela. The neighbors loved Clove's dress style and complimented Charles's skills. While they were catching up on all the gossip, the doorbell rang, this time it was Connor and Camila. All five of them were excited wishing each other a 'Merry Christmas.' Charles took their coats as Chloe ushered them in. Clove was busy digging into the sweet and savory items that Camila had packed.

Charles opened a bottle of wine to serve it to all. After reciting the grace before meals everyone was busy digging into the sumptuous and delicious meal that was prepared by Chloe. There was laughter, singing, and smiles. After the meal, they played dumb charades, the girls won against the boys. It was then that Clove kissed everyone and went up to her room. Meanwhile, the adults gathered around the fireplace, the warmth of the fire made everyone comfortable from the cold outside.

After a while, there was a commotion. Clove could hear indistinguishable sounds. It was as if they were arguing but she had never witnessed such a scene before

'What had happened?' She had to find out herself. She tiptoed down the stairs till she could hear them without being seen.

"When was the appropriate time for you to disclose this?" Charles sounded angry. "It has been a while. I was not sure till I got a good deal on the bakery and the house. Charles come with us I know back there in the city we can make it big. Think about Clove, about her future do you not want the best? How long will you hang out in this town? Or at least send her with us. I will care for her as my own. You very well know that we cannot have our own. While you can, give us Clove I promise you will never regret it," Conner pleaded. Clove's heart was racing fast she did not want to leave her parents, she was happy to be where she was she would miss them both. Charles rejected the idea. He was happy living in the town and did not want to leave. It was his father's house, something that he held dearly. This house had a history, passed down through generations. Not only that, Charles also belonged to a family of tailors. He could not wrap things, sell them, and let go. To this, Connor got up asking Camila to leave. Clove could hear her mother requesting them to stay. But her father did not budge. He was quiet and calm. Connor walked out the door ushering his wife outside, shutting the door behind.

Chole turned to Charles and cried asking what got into him. Why was he so angry? She felt as if he overreacted. It was something he never did. Charles turned, calmly explaining that they met them almost every day but never shared this information and now all they wanted was Clove because they couldn't have their own. Clove and she were everything to him and he would cling to both of them till the last of his breath.

Clove walked back upstairs, she was confused. She did not know how to react almost numb. She loved her parents and wanted to be with them. But at the same time, her thirteen-year-old intellect could not make peace that Connor and Camila could not have children and wanted her instead.

The evening it was turned out to be quiet, no one spoke to each other. Charles smoked, Chole focused on knitting while Clove watched television. They all had an early supper, calling it a day. As Clove lay down in the bed, she whispered a little prayer hoping that things between them got better. She hated the silence it was awfully painful. But she knew she would always make Uncle Connor change his mind. He loved her dearly and she knew things would change for the better. Mom always told her that there were good and troubled times, it is faith that keeps you going through both times.

A week passed, and neither Charles nor Connor spoke. This was the first time that things got awkward. Charles got upset over silly things, Chole always sobbing and Clove was wondering why everyone kept acting weird. Sometimes, she guessed the adults forgot to say sorry but kept reminding the kids to, do so. The following week was even more weird, it was their first New Year when they didn't celebrate instead, Charles was meeting deadlines while Chloe took up pottery class to distract herself Things were mellowed down.

It was late in the evening, and the doorbell rang. Chloe answered, to her surprise, it was Connor and Camila. They settled in the living room. As Clove approached them, she warmly hugged them both, Camila putting an iron ring on her finger; she told Clove that this was her lucky charm and girls in their family wore it she wanted her to have it as a memory, she had engraved

Clove, Connor & Camila. She told her that it should ward off evil at all times and to never take it off. She had got her ginger cookies and promised to send all her favorite stuff later. Clove wished them goodbye, heading to bed. Tears rolled down her eyes, she didn't know why. She heard her Dad and Mom wishing them goodbye while her Mom and Camila were sobbing. She somehow knew they made peace, she guessed that it should do them well. Uncle Connor had finally wound his business, packed his luggage, and sent it ahead by transport. They were hopeful and ready to start a new life in the city but still, they wanted Charles to come along with them.

Chapter 5

Disaster Ahead

It had been four months since Connor and Camilla had left them. Charles was mostly lonely falling to the vices of smoking and drinking. Clove guessed Charles found it difficult that he and Connor never spoke. He missed him dearly. Chloe on the other side busied herself with making pots and decorating them. She had found a new fancy for ignoring to see Charles's pain. It was her way of dealing with pain. She had started to sell her goods now making money. Clove, on the other hand, went to play with Nicole who was Aunt Pamela's granddaughter. Clove didn't understand why Uncle Connor's absence consumed her father. As days passed, he slowly, developed a cough, becoming breathless he neglected his health and food. He lost weight continuing to work tirelessly. Once in a while, they got an email from Camilla. They had finally adjusted to their surroundings and they were doing good. She sent them tarts, cookies, and cakes every week. She also sent a shirt on Charles's birthday and a dress on Chole's. She tried hard to keep the love between their families.

One morning as Clove was getting ready to go to school, she heard her mom's cry for help. She quickly ran down the stairs to find her father lying in a pool of blood. She guessed he had vomited blood. She did not know what to do, but her mother with her presence of mind, shoved a paper towards her with a number on it. She told Clove, it was Connor's number and that she should call him to ask him to come as soon as possible. Meanwhile, she ran over to Patrick the next-door neighbor, they were happy to help. He gave Charles and Chloe a ride to the hospital as fast as he could. Clove nervously dialed the number and heard the telephone connect. She was hoping that she could get through to one of them, after a long time, she heard Uncle Connor's voice, she was tongue-tied, speechless, and could only sob. "Hello! Who is this?" Uncle Connor inquired. "Uncle it's me Clove. Things here are not okay please come soon. Dad was lying in a pool of blood. Mom, Dad, and Uncle Patrick have gone to the hospital," Clove blabbered amidst her sobs. "Oh! My dear Lord! Don't worry just hang in there we are on our way. Papa will be fine. Just be strong." Connor reassured, consoling Clove.

When Clove put the phone down, she felt peace as if she knew things would get better. When life is hard, when you're in pain and suffering those comforting words of people close to your heart are the solace that gives us the strength to fight trials and tribulations with great gusto. Clove knew her father was a fighter. These tough times would get better. The doorbell rang it was Aunt Pamela. She hugged Clove sitting down with her, she had brought a glass of juice with her, and Clove drank it as she needed something to moist her throat, she was hungry since she did not have her breakfast. After a while, the doorbell rang. Aunt Pamela was prompt to attend to it, Father Tony was here, he was there just to check on her. Patrick had informed him, he had been to the hospital to pray for Charles and Chloe. Father Tony gave Clove words of consolation, hope, and faith yet, her eyes were set on the door eagerly waiting for Connor and Camila.

The telephone rang, and Aunt Pamela walked towards it nervously everyone gathered around, they were hoping for good news, it was Connor. He had reached the hospital and Camilla would be joining them shortly. Charles was in the Intensive Care Unit. The doctor had asked Chloe to keep her fingers crossed. The news was not good but Clove would not give up.

The doorbell rang announcing the arrival of Aunt Camila. Tears knew no bounds, just flowing from Cloves' eyes. Camila informed Aunt Pamela that she would be staying with Clove. Aunt Pamela asked her not to cook as she would be sending food over and to the hospital as well. Camila was grateful and thanked Aunt Pamela. Father Tony also left saying he would keep Charles in his prayers knowing that Clove was now in safe hands.

Camila hugged Clove. Clove was wailing, as Camila consoled her. Camila made a cup of hot chocolate for Clove to drink, then proceeded to clean the mess in the house, and called up Clove's principal at school, informing her about Clove's absence.

She did all the chores of the house, by then it was lunchtime. Aunt Pamela got them lunch informing them Uncle Matt; her son, had left lunch for Chloe and Connor at the hospital on his way to work, so far nothing much had changed. She left them to have lunch.

Clove's mind was racing although she was hoping, hearing only negative reports humbly asked Camila, "I want to meet Dad, this is driving me crazy, I have so much to tell him! Can you take me to him?" Camila replied, "Yes sweetheart, I am here to take care of you. We shall meet him during visiting hours. I will take you myself in the evening. But before that, I want you to get good sleep." They somehow just gulped down the food, by now both had lost their appetite. Camila held Clove in her arms as she lay with Clove in bed. Clove felt safe and cared for, and both drifted away to sleep.

The telephone rang waking them up. It was Chloe, and Clove answered it. "Honey, Dad is being shifted to the Operation Room there is massive bleeding in the lungs. I would want you to meet him, he wants to see you." Chole was, requesting. "We are on our way, Mom. Do you need anything?" To which Chloe replied, "No honey, just come." Aunt Camila was ready, and both hurried to the hospital. Camila went to park the car while Conner came down to receive them. He took them straight to where Charles was. The nurse requested them to meet him one at a time. Clove was the first to go, she saw a lot of tubes attached to her dad, and she had tears in her eyes. She had always seen her father up and about, and to see him tied down in tubes broke her heart. "Daddy, how are you? You look quite weak," Clove asked. "Honey, I am breathless. I want you to know I love you. Please take care of Mom. Hold on to what is good. If I survive this, we will build your tree house; always remember I love that Oak tree in the backyard never let mom cut it; It is priceless to me." Charles spoke in his delirium. Chloe followed in as the nurses started to shift him. "Honey, it's going to be ok. I love you." Chloe was calm, and strong but anxious, all at the same time. She would not cry to make him weak. Charles held on to her," Honey, I am sorry. I may not make it. Take care of Clove and stay happy, please, keep the Oak tree." He coughed more blood, falling unconscious.

The nurses rushed him to the Operation Room. They all sat in the hallway waiting for something positive, Connor got everyone coffee. The wait was killing. Chole wondered why Charles asked for forgiveness. He was a good husband and a father. He had kept them happy and catered to their needs. If all it was her turn to apologize, she was so self-engrossed with her business that she had missed the signs.

"Mrs. Chloe." The doctor approached her breaking her chain of thoughts." "Yes, that's me." "Madam, we tried our best. Mr. Charles is no more, I am sorry for your loss. We will try our best to release the body as soon as we can." Before the doctor could complete his sentence, Chloe collapsed. Connor caught her right in time, she was crying. Charles was no more. The love of her life was no more. His face flashed in front of her. His last words were echoing in Chloe's mind. She was numb, not responding to anyone. She saw their entire life fast-forward before her. He had left her too soon.

Chloe closed her eyes. Now, it was just Clove and herself. This was the time Charles would want her to be strong but she could not comprehend a life without him. It would be difficult but she had to endure it for Clove reaching out for Clove, she hugged her. She was seeing Charles in her. Charles was living through Clove and the memories that they made together. "Oh! Charles, why did you go so soon?" Chloe muttered in despair.

Chapter 6

Goodbyes

"Dearly beloved, we are gathered here today to pray for our dead and departed soul of Brother Charles Campbell. Thank you, everyone, for making it at such short notice. Charles was well known as a friendly, warm, companionate, and generous individual. He was attached to his family and friends. I don't think that we would have ever heard him raise his voice. He was a good tailor as it was his family business. He worked hard out doing what his grandfather and father could do together.

Charles is survived by his beloved wife Chloe Campbell, who is an entrepreneur and has her own pottery business, and his only daughter Clove Campbell, a bright student pursuing her studies at St. Mary's School. Charles was very close to his best friends Conner and Camila Burns, they were his partners in crime and they were with him in his final moments; a pillar of strength to Mrs. Chloe Campbell.

Charles was always optimistic. I would like to narrate an incident. It was Easter, I was at his shop to stitch a shirt. The material which I brought was in excess. So, he asked me if I would like to keep it or donate it so that some poor boy would get a new shirt. He made an offer; he promised to reduce his charges if I would leave the material. I took the offer and for Easter vigil, I saw a boy play in the courtyard at mass in a shirt with the same leftover fabric. Indeed, he was a living Santa for so many of us. No wonder the Church hall is packed today. I have not seen a crowd like this before. Charles was a god-fearing man, a devout Christian, he was strong-footed in faith and his family too imbibed it.

The Charles I know would want you to be happy at all times. He always believed that happiness is from within not what we pin on worldly things. With this, I end my tribute to Brother Charles. May his soul rest in peace and his family have the strength to bear his loss. Chloe, you have my prayers and support." Patrick stepped down, marking the end of his eulogy. Patrick was with him in his last moments, he had admitted him with Chloe at the hospital as a neighbor, and they knew each other well.

Chloe and Clove were seated in the hall near Charles's photograph, there were white lilies placed in a vase in front of his photograph with lit white candles on a globe. It had been a week since they had buried him, Chloe had arranged a prayer service and get-together for family & friends at the Church Hall. Chloe and Clove have been visiting his grave every day, it was as if they were stuck. All who knew Charles were there for his funeral. Those who could not make it were here today to pay their last respects. Life was difficult for Chloe and Clove to wake up, not seeing him around.

Connor and Camila were a big help, Connor took care of all the arrangements and Camila took care of the house chores so Chloe could grieve her husband's death in peace. Connor and Clove were working on the tree house that Charles wanted to build; Connor wanted to build it as it was Charles's last wish, he was on a mission to complete everything that was left incomplete. The workers in the tailoring shop completed their orders. Chloe had not gone to work but her assistants took care of the pottery business.

Camila was looking for house help. Chloe will need all the help she can get. Camila and Connor would leave in two days, they were looking for reliable people to take care of Clove while Chloe was working and supervising the tailoring business as well.

"Chloe dear, it's time to go home. The guests have eaten and left. Nobody disturbed you, Clove met everyone and took care. She reminds me of Charles. Would you like to eat something or shall we wind up?" Connor asked Chloe. "No, I am fine. Camila did bring me coffee. Aunt Pamela got me a plate when food was served. Let's wrap up, I want to go home, please." Chloe replied. "Very well then. Camila will drive you folks' home. I will make the payments and meet Father Tony, clear all dues if that's okay with you," Connor asked. "That's fine with me," Connor informed Camila to do the needful, all three were on their way back home.

The entire ride back all Chloe thought was, that there were so many people whose lives were touched by Charles. He had helped many and now people just kept coming to meet them, some brought food, some brought flowers, and some offered help. Clove and Chloe were overwhelmed with the love and affection people had showered on them. Charles had earned a lifetime of support for them in addition to the financial security he had built.

Camila parked the car, opening the front door for all to enter. "Chloe, I want you to change, I have called people here to interview them, as before I go I need to find you a house help. Patrick recommended them let us see if they fit in right," Camila said. She had barely finished saying this, and the doorbell rang. "You speak of the devil and the devil appears or should I say angel in our case. You change and freshen up while I take a head start," saying this, Camila walked to open the front door while Chloe walked towards the stairs, reaching the foot of the stairs. There was a commotion at the front door, and the murmuring of voices caught Chloe's attention. She felt that she had heard a man's voice which she was familiar with even though, it was quite faint. Chloe retraced her steps back to the front door as she was getting closer to the door the voices were starting to get audible. The next thing she knew the voice was none other than her father's, her eyes widened and her mouth opened wide; what did he want from her? Charles was gone. She wished he were there. It was thirteen years since she left home and walked down the aisle. He had told her that she was dead for him. Why did he come after so many years? What could bring him here? These thoughts were racing through her mind as she approached the door. She suddenly felt the strength within her grow, she calmed herself opening the front door wide signaling Camila to move from the way.

"Yes, Mr. Raven Murray how can I help you? What brings you here at my doorstep after thirteen long years?" Chloe asked, angrily. "I know Chloe you are angry and grieving the biggest loss of your life but can you hear me out? At least child, for old-time sake?" Her father pleaded with her. "Very well then please make it quick," Chloe said calmly, ushering her father inside the house. "Camila, could you please bring us something to eat and please ask Clove to be upstairs until I call for her." Camila nodded her head in agreement and walked towards the kitchen.

The drawing room had a big picture of Charles smiling. They had clicked the picture on Christmas. He was looking his best; Chloe wanted his smiling picture so they could draw inspiration; that is how she wanted him to be remembered. There were candles lit before it, red roses were placed in a vase between the candles. It was afternoon the sunlight entered the room through the French window, the entire room was bathed in the sunlight. Chloe asked her dad to sit across the table on the couch so she would sit face to face to hear him out. Chloe was determined not to be moved by anything he said. Although, in her heart, she just wanted to cry out aloud and hug him. All these years she wanted her father to accept Charles and see him through her eyes. Deep in her heart, she knew that he would have loved him. Anyone could love him; he was such a lovely human being, and none had a different opinion. Alas! The train was missed. Charles was gone. It had taken his death to bring her father to her. She was not willing to bail out on Charles. She had never done it when he was alive and she would not do it even more now after his death.

Her father sat teary eye in front of her though he was unable to meet her eyes. He looked guilty and weak at the same time. He had aged. He had gotten dark eye circles, and gone bald, wrinkles around the eyes were evident. He had lost weight.

Chapter 7

The Reunion

Camila came with a coffee tray, ginger cookies, and chicken puffs. She laid it on the table between them and served Mr. Raven and Chloe. She moved out of the room, giving them privacy, and to check on Clove who was in her room upstairs.

"I saw the Obituary of Charles in the paper. I called Connor and he filled me in" Mr. Raven was the first to speak breaking the icy cold silence between them. "You called Connor? How did you get his number?" Inquired Chloe.

"Six months back I met Connor in a mall in the city. He was looking for a place to rent or buy for his bakery. I asked him to come to my office, which he did. I made him an offer," Mr. Raven responded.

"What offer are you talking about?" "Well, I told him if he could get Charles to move here to the city along with you people, I would gift him a hefty deal. I would buy his bakery and settle him down." "Oh! that's why he was behind our blood. That hurt Charles. Papa, you killed my husband." Chloe accused in anger, standing up. "Hold your horses! Connor spat on my face. He turned down the offer, and he told me that if Charles ever moved here it would be because of the love for them as they are a family. Not because I wanted to. Moreover, he said he despised me for how I treated you both. He never wanted to do anything with me, he just came over to see if I asked about you and my granddaughter," Mr. Raven was defensive, on his feet just like Chloe. "If this is true then we can sit down and talk like civilized human beings," by saying so she gestured for him to sit down.

"So, tell me why you are here. Why did you want us to move to the city?" asked Chloe, not missing eye contact with her father. She was judging his reply. "I am afraid it's your mom." Mr. Raven was interrupted by "What happened to her?" "When you left us, it was like the happiness left. Mom was dealing with her grief silently. I was channeling my anger through work. James your brother joined the priesthood, Charlotte, your younger sister is no more." "What? When did this happen?" "She was diagnosed with ovarian cancer and we came to know quite late we took her to the U.S. but we lost her. It's six months now. Your mom felt lonely, she has grown silent nowadays. She only cries. I couldn't see her pain. So, I called Charles." "You did what? Called my husband?" Chloe yelled. "I did. Connor got a good deal with my rival company, that's when I met him for the second time and that's when he told me about Clove. I saw her picture in Connor's purse. Connor told me that he had put in a word with Charles, but he had declined. I called Charles when we lost Emma your sister. I apologized to him, I begged him to come to the funeral or send you and Clove over. I sent some office guys over from the city to meet him regularly. They got him home once, but he said, "We cannot mend ways. I can forgive you, but you will have to keep a distance. I do not wish to do anything with you." "I don't believe you," Chloe was shocked covering her face, mumbling. "Ask Connor, if you trust him because he is a witness to my story," said Mr. Raven.

"I don't know who to trust. I can't understand why Charles would do this. I cannot comprehend why Connor would hide these things from me." Chloe was muttering

"Darling, I made a mistake. Please forgive me. Give me a chance for atonement. I want to care for you and Clove that is all we have and I want to hold on to you," Mr. Raven was pleading with his daughter. "Dad, what took you so long? I cannot trust you anymore. I need some time to think." Chloe implored. "Alright, I will come after two days. I am willing to accept whatever you decide." Mr. Raven offered, walking out in tears. A devastated Chloe sat in the drawing room not knowing who to believe. Then, Charles' last words rang in her head *'I am sorry …I am sorry …I am sorry.'* Was he apologizing for not making peace between them? She wanted answers from Connor. She was hoping for the truth, nothing less than the truth. The doorbell rang, and she walked to get it as she opened it; Connor was back. "I cleared all the dues and when we were vacating the hall. I met a lady who approached me. She asked about Clove and you, she needed work and shared her experience with Charles. He had helped her; she had come to repay the loan that Charles had lent her during her grim times. She sounded genuine and was willing to take care of you both so, I called her to meet you in the evening. You can interview her if you like," Connor said, moving towards the drawing room. Seeing the snacks laid before, he asked Chloe who followed after, "Did we have guests?" "Yes, as a matter of fact, we did. But I need some explanation from you and this time you will not hide the truth from me, you will tell me everything you know." Chloe was looking into Connor's eyes without blinking, she had meant every word of what she said. "Chloe, are you serious? This is me you are talking about! What's the matter?" Connor replied, surprised. "My dad was here; he said a few things that surprised me." "Look I do not know what he said to you but I can tell you whatever I know, there is nothing to hide." Chloe interrupted, "I want to know if you have been speaking to him. How long have you been doing so? What did you two speak behind my back?"

Conner ushered her to sit down as he sat opposite her. He started to narrate the six-month-long ordeal with her father, Connor looked at Chloe and said, "I don't know what Uncle Raven said but, I have a right to my side of the story and I want you to patiently hear me out. I think it could be eight months back. Camila and I went to the city where we live now to look for adoption. Yes, we thought let us adopt a baby so we went to an orphanage. When we went there we looked at all the kids and we had taken stuff from the bakery for the orphanage. But somehow, we were not satisfied with any child, we were so attached to Clove that we were trying to see bits of Clove in every kid. But Clove is special and unique, we cannot have another. We came back after some days and forgot all about it. After a while, we got a call from the orphanage stating that a philanthropist had visited the orphanage and had tasted our puffs, and wanted us to have a branch in the city; something like a franchise. Camila was against it but I wanted to hear them out. So, I secretly went to the city. The guy asked me to meet him in a mall. When I was there waiting for him, I saw your dad for the first time. We met and he asked me to come over to his office, I was very sure that I didn't want to do business with him yet I still went to his office. He gave me a very lucrative offer. He would pay for my house and bakery so that I would have funds to go solo in the city. Unfortunately, he wanted Charles, you, and Clove to settle in the city with him even if you choose to live separately. The entire conversation, I felt it was all about him and nothing had changed so I spat, turning the offer down. I just walked out. "Conner continued. "Meanwhile, I met Mr. Smith he is a young and dynamic businessman; his offer was better so, I took it. I thought why not go and start afresh? I told him about Charles and he said he was willing to do business with both. He would need a dress code for the employees and Charles could do the needful." Conner continued as Chloe listened. "When I came back I told this to Charles, he was not too keen but he wanted to know about the terms and conditions. He wanted to be doubt-free. So, before he could decide, he asked me to keep this a secret. We both went to the city to meet up with Mr. Smith. The meeting did go well. Charles had made up his mind to switch. Things took a turn when I met your dad for a second time, which I regret dearly. I went to him and informed him about my deal though I never told him about Charles's decision. I told them that he wasn't in favor. But, I wanted him to know about Clove so I showed him her picture and he was happy to know about her, and wanted to meet her. For the first time, I saw his genuine feelings for Clove. I thought to myself that I would be able to unite you with your family. The next time I went for the advance, I came to know about Emma, Uncle Raven wanted you folks to come for the funeral. So, I gave him Charles's number and your dad spoke to him. They spoke but Charles never filled me in. For the first time, I saw him angry, which changed his mind to move uptown." Chloe interrupted, "Oh my God! I cannot believe this." Conner did not pause and kept going, "After that, Charles was distant. He lied outright, before you. But I had given him a man's word so I never spoke of it until now. He is dead. But I know things changed after that phone call that your dad made. The only way we know the truth is by playing along with Mr. Raven. Now after Charles is gone, I'm curious to know what happened." Conner ended his confession. "Well, most of your story matched with what I have heard so I know you are telling me the truth but, what I can't comprehend is why Charles would hide or lie to me. Why would he hide my sister's funeral from me? This has to be big; the only way is to know from my mom. I know she would tell me, so I will have to go home." Chloe exhaled as she spoke. She had a lot to take in a day.

Connor warned Chloe, "Let the past rest, please don't go back. You have sufficient and more. You have us. Just let it go for the love of God. Give me time. The truth will only give you a heartache." Chloe had tears in her eyes, "I need to know the truth. I need answers. Charles is not here to give it to me and I will go to the root of this." Chloe sobbed she felt betrayed and helpless, all at once but she was determined to know what happened and why Charles hid things from her. There had to be something huge and this was something that was the need of the hour.

"Connor, I have made my mind up. I want you to stick with me. I have to get to the bottom of this. We are going to the city. I will be at my father's residence. We will keep in touch. Please keep this to yourself; keep Camila and Clove out of it. I want them to be ignorant so we don't give an alibi." Chloe pleaded with Connor as he finally gave in.

Chapter 8

Family Meeting

"Why can't we stay at Uncle Connor's? I do not know them." Clove complained, "All the better reason to stay at grandmas." Chloe said locking all the rooms upstairs, walking downstairs, Clove following Chloe down.

Connor and Camila had packed their bags waiting for Clove and Chloe. They had paid the workers two months in advance and given instructions to continue work. Meanwhile, Connor would come and supervise them in between. The packing for Clove and Chloe was done. The housekeepers were finalized and told to join after two months or for any further changes, they would be informed.

All four were waiting for Mr. Raven to send a car to pick them up. Chloe had called her father and he was pleased to hear that she had changed her mind. He was grateful that she was willing to consider living with them. Her mom and he were looking forward to meeting Clove for the first time and were all excited to welcome her to their place.

It was nine in the morning; the driver would be here any minute everyone getting restless. The doorbell rang, and Connor went to attend to it. It was the driver, "I am here to pick up Mrs. Chloe Campbell and Ms. Clove Campbell, Mr. Donald will help with the luggage shifting." Connor shook his head saying, "Very well, kindly let Donald come in and do the needful." Connor ushered him in helping with the loading of the luggage, when it was finished, they all stood in the drawing room in front of Charles's picture each silently saying their goodbyes. It was like they all felt his presence here and now, all felt they were leaving him behind, it would not be for long though yet, the heart still did ache.

Chloe and Clove sat in the vehicle sent by Mr. Raven. At the same time, Connor and Camila followed them in theirs. Mr. Donald and Clove were happily chatting in the car teasing and playing games. As they crossed, Mr. Donald showed Clove the forest, speaking about its flora and fauna. He had made Clove comfortable and they were getting to know each other better. Chloe was pensive, silently sitting and watching the view from the window.

"Wow! This is so huge!" exclaimed Clove as the car entered the mansion. "You will like it here. There is a swimming pool and a garden which has a swing. Your mom and aunt always used to swing when they were little and you will do so now." Mr. Donald said

Chloe's mother, Rebecca was at the entrance waiting to receive them. As she saw Clove she knelt and opened her arms. Chloe walked towards her, introducing Clove to her grandmother. Rebecca's warm embrace melted away the anxiety in Clove's heart she never had experienced her grandparents' love but, there are always firsts to experience in life.

Rebecca introduced Elizabeth, she would be her governess and would take care of Clove during her stay there. Clove was happy with the attention that she got and quickly ran off with Mr. Donald and Elizabeth to have a quick tour of the mansion.

"Oh, my darling! I have missed you so much. It's been ages since I have seen you," Mrs. Rebecca hugged her daughter saying these warm words. "Come let's sit in the parlor, I will ring in for someone to bring us coffee. Do not worry Mr. Donald will take care of the luggage. Let's just chill I am so happy you are here." Rebecca held Chloe's hand as she spoke walking towards the parlor.

Chloe's phone rang and she stopped to get it from the bag. It was Connor he had called to inform her that he and Camilla had reached safely. They invited them over for dinner today so they could both check out their place. Chloe said she would confirm with them in a while as she had to check if her mom had other plans. She then hung up to join her mother in the parlor.

"How are you dear? Life has been hard on you, first the poverty, then Charles leaving, my baby has gone through a lot." Rebecca had tears in her eyes. "Mom, Charles unlike Dad was a loving, caring husband. We faced difficulties together, yet my life has been very kind. I had lovely warm in-laws. They were our pillars of strength. Charles had kept his wedding vows. I have no regrets. My only regret is that he left me soon. I wish that we had more time together." Chloe answered her, sternly. Meanwhile, the coffee and some biscuits were placed before them. "Nonsense! I know you deserved more. What are your plans now? Have you given it a thought? You have an entire life ahead. You certainly cannot be thinking of living alone." Rebecca sipped her cup of coffee as she schooled her daughter. "I have Clove and that's more than enough. I have Charles's love to last me a lifetime. I am happy and let me live in peace. If it is not up to your taste, I am willing to return from where I came." Chloe was serious looking straight in her mother's eye making each word clear to her.

"Oh! You just came and now you want to go. I just wanted to know your stance. Please, I apologize. On a lighter side, we have kept a welcome party today for you and Clove. Just neighbors and Dad's business friends. I hope you are not too tired," Rebecca asked. "No, it's fine. Can I call Connor and Camila too? Clove would like them over. They called me for dinner but I would like them to come over. If it's fine with you." Chloe suggested. "Nonsense! this is your house do and live as you like," Rebecca exclaimed. "Go freshen up and change, lunch will be served in a while." Rebecca got up and walked her to her room. "Oh! Mom it's exactly like I left it." Chloe was amazed and happy to be in her room. It gave her a chirpy mood after a long time. "Clove is settled in Emma's room. Across the hall, I thought it would be nice if your rooms were close by." Rebecca mentioned. "Yes, Mom indeed that would be nice." Rebecca showed Chloe Clove's room. The room was redecorated for Clove it had soft toys, and pastel shades and the furniture matched the color theme. "I think Clove will love it. You have indeed outdone yourself." Chloe blurted out the words in excitement.

"Very well, I leave you to rest. But not for long. Elizabeth and I will take care of Clove. Come down for lunch, I'll meet you there." Rebecca stated, on her way downstairs.

Chloe called Connor to invite them over for dinner. She wanted them by her side as several unfamiliar faces would make her nervous. Connor promised to be there though, they would be late as they would be visiting the bakery and the workers. Chloe was not hungry, she wanted to lie down in her bed, so she took off her shoes and got into it. Before she knew it, she was fast asleep.

"Mom, wake up! it's me Clove, aren't you getting ready for the party?" Clove was trying to wake her mother up. "What time is it?" Chloe inquired. "It's six in the evening. Hurry up!" Clove exclaimed, ticking her mother. "Someone's all excited. I wonder why?" smiling Chloe asked her daughter. "I love parties and will be making new friends! Much more exciting!" Exclaimed Clove.

Chloe smiled she had not seen Clove so excited in a while, she thought to herself that maybe the party would do them good. Mr. Donald brought her a bowl of fruits, sandwiches, and tea which she happily gobbled down as she had skipped lunch because she had slept in the entire afternoon. Chloe dressed in a white blouse & black skirt, wore red lipstick and light makeup, tying her hair in a bun.

She looked great. It had been a while since she had dressed well. She was back home all excited that a new chapter was beginning that she was looking forward to.

Chapter 9

Welcome Party

"There you are, honey! You look great! Welcome home. Sorry, I was not there. Caught up at work. I love you." Mr. Raven hugged his daughter Chloe. Chloe was smiling. No matter the differences between her father and her, hugs are contagious and can bring a smile to anyone's face. "I told you the change will do her and me good," Rebecca spoke bringing Clove along. "My little munchkin! There's lots to do! We have to go fishing and every Saturday is planned." Mr. Raven said, placing an arm around his granddaughter Clove and kissing her.

The hall was well-lit with candles on the stand, a huge chandelier in the middle of the room added to the warmth, flower vases had a purple & white theme, and the smell of the flowers was enchanting. The furniture was along three sides of the room, the center was vacant for couples to dance. Food was displayed at one end of the hall. There was a banner put up saying, "Welcome home! Clove and Chloe."

The first guest to arrive was Brother James Murray; he was Chloe's brother and partner in crime. "Chloe! It's so good to see you and my lovely niece!" He hugged them both. Tears of joy were rolling down his cheeks. "Me too bro! Oops! Brother James," Chloe replied, embarrassed. "Nay! I am and will be your little bro," replied James. "I am home for 15 days, then I will have to go back," James added. "That is great we can, you know, spend some time together," Chloe commented. Then, James went to meet his parents, and the hugs and greetings just followed.

One by one, the guests started to enter, and soon the hall was crowded. The kids had their party in the neighboring room and were watched over by the governess including other attendees. The list included Mr. Henry Walsh and his family, the immediate neighbors of the Murray family, Uncle George Murray, Mr. Raven's younger brother, Aunty Cathy Collins, and her family, Mrs. Rebecca's elder sister, Mr. Arthur Quinn and family, Mr. Raven Murray's business associate, lastly Mr. Karl Byrne and his family, their close family friends.

The music was playing, there was dancing. Clove was dancing with her newfound Uncle. Chloe was surrounded by the ladies who sympathized with her at her loss, few applauded her for her business sense, stating she had it in her genes. Some wanted her to settle down again. Chloe felt suffocated, she needed a savior. Her eyes were scanning the room when she heard someone speak from behind, "Looking for me?" Conner said, extending his hand forward in the hope of getting a dance with Chloe, Chloe responded with a smile, "Your entry was indeed dramatic." They proceeded to the dance floor, Chloe was first to break the silence asking, "Where is Camila?" "At home, you know she hates crowds. Moreover, she had a headache from the journey. I let her rest. I must say you look great! The weight loss has done you good. You look rather ravishing." Conner smiled as he spoke. "Ravishing! Oh my God! The last time you said I was 'ravishing' was when you proposed to me in college and I turned you down." Chloe laughed. "Watch out madam, I am happily married and I have a lovely niece! That was way before Charles had joined college." Connor rolled his eyes as he spoke. Chloe was laughing at his antics as the song came to an end. Clove ran over to her

Uncle Connor asking him for a dance this time. "See madam, I am very loved and appreciated by ladies of all ages," Connor remarked proudly. "Ouch! I can hear the donkey praise himself." Chloe said before fleeing their presence. Chloe could see both of them smiling from the corner of her eyes. She was headed towards her aunt but was interrupted by her father. "Chloe I would love to introduce you to Mr. Philip Smith. He is a young dynamic and emerging business tycoon. He did his master's in the U.S. and came down to join his family business. He has a chain of hotels and restaurants. He wants to venture into construction like us. I told him my daughter is an entrepreneur and you must give her some tips," Saying this Mr. Raven gave them privacy to get acquainted.

"I guess your dad painted a very fancy picture of me. I am not so great. So, what can I offer the lady Champagne or a dance?" Mr. Smith asked. "I had a lot of wine and I danced with my friend. I rather would have a walk in the garden. If that's ok with you. I just want to be in a quiet place away from all the noise with someone who doesn't judge me. Do not worry I do not bite, you will be safe with me." Chloe winked at Mr. Smith walking towards the exit. A shocked Mr. Smith followed her with a smile on his face.

He met her at the entrance, silently walking away from the gathering. The music slowly faded away, the cool breeze flowing against their faces. Mr. Smith took off his coat and tie, folding his pants making his way towards the swing. Both sat on either side facing each other. Initially, the conversation revolved around the party and guests, Chloe was filling in on her childhood and the fun she had in the garden. Mr. Smith laughed occasionally; both soon they were comfortable with each other.

"Chloe, I wanted to do business with you." Mr. Smith was looking straight into her eyes as he continued to speak. "I don't know if you spoke to Connor or your dad. I do business with Connor he supplies all the bakery, desserts, and confectionary items to my chain of hotels and restaurants. I must say he is good and very professional. It was in his outlet that I saw designer pots on display with indoor plants. When I inquired, I got to know they were gifts from you. Could we work out something together? I want to decorate one of my outlets with such pots and if I like what I see then, the other outlets can be roped in." Smith was looking for confirmation from Chloe. "Thank you for the appreciation and yes, I would like to do business with you," Chloe confirmed. "Well, let me have the honor of lunch with you tomorrow," Mr. Smith proposed. "Excuse me? Are you hitting on me?" Chloe questioned. "No! Chloe, I just thought you would see the place, taste the food, and get creative," Mr. Smith was quick to reply. "I was just joking!" Chloe said, smiling. "I guess you got to me." Mr. Smith smiled.

"Are you back to kindergarten?" Connor asked both of them. They missed his arrival in the dark as both of them were discussing their business plans. "They want you to cut the cake and the grace before meals have to be said. If you don't turn in this very minute. The police will be informed and a search party will be summoned." Connor informed Chole, adding humor to the information.

To which, both of them arose and walked towards the gathering. The cake was cut by Clove and Chloe; she fed a piece of cake to her parents, brother, and Connor. Dinner was served, everyone had food, and the guests slowly dispersed. Clove was put to bed by her governess, only the family members were left in the hall. The servants were clearing the room as all sat sipping their coffee.

"Chloe, there is a school nearby. It's good. Mr. Henry put in a good word for us. Their grandson Clarke is also in the eighth grade. Why don't you look at the brochure? If it is up to your expectations, I would love to get the admission done. Clove will have company," Saying this her dad placed the brochure in Chloe's hand. "Dad, I have spoken with the principal at St. Mary's. She is a good student and they have been very kind after what we have gone through. At Connor's request, she would have to go to take her final exams. Meanwhile, they have given us the list of chapters. I have already given it to Elizabeth. In that case, let's think of transfer next year." Chloe responded to her dad's suggestion as she yawned. "Very well, that settles it. Rebecca dear, the party was lovely." Mr. Raven remarked.

Later, Mr. Raven and Mrs. Rebecca went upstairs to get some rest. As Chloe got up to walk upstairs her brother James caught her hand pulling her towards him, "What's with the garden and Mr. Smith? You need to fill me in." James looked for some positive gossip, but a sleepy Chloe just crushed his hopes by saying, "Strictly business."

Chapter 10

Business Lunch

"I must say you are punctual Chloe." Mr. Philip Smith wore a suit to work. Today, he wore a chocolate-colored, double-breasted suit with a white shirt. He was tall somewhere around 5 feet and 11 inches, he had a prominent jawline with hazel eyes, he had black hair, a well-trimmed French beard, and a fair complexion. If he walked passed you, you would give him a second look.

"Work ethics, I love to be on time," Chloe responded. Chloe was wearing a red business suit with a white shirt and had worn red lipstick. She looked great and her confidence was in seventh heaven. This deal was huge. If he liked her work, it would take her business to another level and she was sure he would bring along a boom of clients for her, she had to be at her best to win the contract.

"Let us have lunch. I am starving," He picked up the menu as he continued speaking. "Hey! Are you a vegan or a lamb chops girl?" "Well, definitely not vegan." "Do you fancy anything on the menu?" "Since you are the boss, I would like to choose the best on the menu. You are aware of what is good here." Chloe said resting her back on the chair. "Very well! Kindly, call Edmond please," Mr. Smith asked the attending waiter to invite the Chef to the table. "Sir, you called for me?" The Chef asked. "Yes, I did. Meet Mrs. Chloe Campbell, we have called her here to decorate this place with her pots and she is skilled in her art. I want her to taste the absolute best so that the taste creates a lasting impression to stimulate her creativity." All three laughed at the comment. "It is a pleasure to have you here Madam, I will try my absolute best to please you. Do you have any allergies or any special requests?" "Oh! Not really. I love to have great food. So, surprise me." Chloe responded as the conversation ended with, the chef thanking them, politely leaving them to their devices.

"That was quick. Well, I don't know why you want to change it. It is all beautifully decorated" Chloe looked into his eyes, seeking clarity. "Have you heard of Simon O'Neill, the chef?" "Yes, the one who died in a car accident last year?" Chloe questioned. "She was my wife." Mr. Smith had tears in his eyes. Chloe's jaw dropped in response. "We had an arranged cum love marriage. My dad played Cupid. Dad had started with this very restaurant hiring her as the chef. I was in the U.S. back then and on my holiday trips, I would sometimes have a difference of opinion with the menu, dad always supported her, and trusted her gut instincts. I hate to admit but she was good at her job, I was good at expanding my business; one thing led to the other and before we knew it, we were in love even happily married! One fateful night, the driver of the opposite vehicle was drunk and the car rammed into a tree at the side of the road. Dad ended up in a wheelchair and we lost her forever. The driver died on the spot. Later, I came to know that she was pregnant. She died without knowing the news. In one night, I lost my unborn child and my dear wife." He closed his eyes, tears rolling down his cheeks, and he bowed his head down gently. Chloe reached out, pressing his hand gently. He placed his hands over hers in acknowledgment. He continued, "She had decorated this place, every single day that I come here I think of her. I want to let go. I want to be free." He raised his head as he spoke.

The waiter brought along the first course, house homemade soup of the day with sourdough toast this indeed was good enough to bring them back to the present time. Gradually, the food started to work its magic as the courses followed, the heavily charged emotions slowly disappeared and the mood eased a little. They got to know each other better. They had one thing in common both had lost the love of their lives at an early age. They were finding a common thread, the silent grief that each was enduring. At least Chloe had Clove, he had his work only.

"Hey! There you are. What took you so long? "an excited Clove asked her mom. She continued, "Grandpa arranged for fishing today. We caught a salmon in the sea. Uncle James made Grandma cook it on the boat. Mom, Grandma is a pro. I loved her salmon." "Was it better than mine?" asked Chloe. "Hmmm! Let me think. A hundred percent." Clove ran upstairs afraid of being caught by her mother. "You guys went on a fishing trip and didn't bother to inform me." Chloe asked her mom, irritated. "You had a business lunch and Clove was bored, James is here and you know he loves fresh fish. Dad was free, it was decided in the spur of the moment. How was the lunch?" her mother inquired. Chloe raised her eyebrow held her hand to her forehead and replied "Emotionally charged."

"What does that mean? Did you get the contract?" Rebecca tried to ask, as she saw her daughter climb up the stairs leaving her puzzled. "Yes, I got it. Emotionally charged because he is going through what I am to cut the story short. Now spare me the horror of the details. I need to make a couple of calls." Saying this, she had disappeared into the hallway, Mrs. Rebecca not wanting to pester her any further walked away too.

Chloe entered to check on Clove, who was fast asleep. Definitely after her boat trip, why wouldn't she? Her governess Mrs. Elizabeth was in the room. Chloe enquired about her thanking her for the wonderful job she was doing. She thought of taking Clove to Camilla & Connor's house in the evening, a lot was going on and she had not been to their place yet. That way, they all could have fun. She walked outside the room across the hallway and headed towards her room she threw her bag and file on her bed pulling out her phone. She tried calling Camilla but did not get an answer. She called Conner, and he received the phone. "Hello, where are you folks? Camilla is not picking up my call." "Chloe, I am in the hospital, Camilla fainted today for now, and the doctors are running some tests, I am really scared, I hope it's not something big." Connor was panicking. "I am on my way," Chloe responded. "No dear, why don't you do me a favor? Can you come in the evening with Clove? That would cheer her up. She has been sulking lately," Connor requested "Should I bring something to eat?" "No, it's been taken care of" "Ok! See you in the evening." Chloe hung up.

After a while Chloe's phone rang once more but this time it was Arthur Bannon, her assistant. "Yes! Arthur, what is it?" "I am sorry to disturb you, madam but the matter is urgent." "What is it, Arthur?" "Madam, the tailoring business is on the decline. We need orders. The sales are at an all-time low. We have a pending assignment for approval. If we get it then, I don't see any need to worry. If you could do something about it?" "Whose is it?" "It Black Orchid Inc., Mr. Philip Smith's. Sir Charles was planning on expansion we had sent the quotations and designs for their staff office wear. They said they would let us know but the scenario changed as we lost sir. Before we hear from them can you pursue it for us? Is it fine with you or should I come for help?"

asked Arthur "In this regard, I was to call you, I have got a huge order for the pots in the pipeline. I think I can follow up with Mr. Smith. Can you give me time? Camila is admitted and unwell. I don't know what is wrong with her. I will visit her in the evening and let you know in a few days?" "Oh! That's settled then. I will check on you next week for the designs on of the pots," Arthur thanked her, cutting the call.

Chloe lay on the bed thinking about what was happening. Camila was sick. Charles's business was in the dumps, was it the wrong move to be back? It felt good to be home. She had missed all the love and attention all these years. It was like a dream come true. She slowly drifted into a deep sleep, the bed felt cozy.

Chapter 11

The Hospital Visit

"Mr. Connor, we are doing the best we can. I want to let you know that she is in the third stage of ovarian cancer; this is due to all the fertility treatments that she has endured, I will ask the gynecologic oncologist to give an expert opinion. Surgery and chemotherapy can cure most of the ovarian cancer. Dr. Sabrina will look into it and advise the following treatment plan. She will be in the hospital." Dr. Edward was counseling Connor. He had been, devastated to hear about Camilla's cancer. Yes, she had gone through a lot of fertility treatment back in their initial years of marriage but that would be ten years ago.

Connor thought that the schedule, work pressure, and emotional stress were tiring her down. The odd food timing was doing all the bloating. Today, she had pain in the abdomen causing her to pass out. All this was taking time to sink in, the doctors were hopeful of her recovery with the surgery and chemotherapy but it all depended on how she was going to take the news.

Connor was happy to see Chloe and Clove at the hospital. Clove went to meet her aunt Camila while Connor told Chloe about what Dr. Edward said. Chloe was shocked and Connor was in tears. Chloe asked him to be strong for Camila, they washed their faces before they went to meet Camila.

"And they all lived happily ever after," Said Clove. She had just read her favorite storybook *Cinderella*. Clove loved to read to her aunt and Camila too loved to read to her. She had put Aunty Camila to sleep. Seeing Connor and Chloe enter, she signaled them to not make noise. She had her finger on her lips. Clove believed that there was magic and she knew she had a fairy Godmother when the time would be ideal she would appear. Connor and Chloe left Clove with Camila and sat outside waiting for her to wake up. Chloe was the first to break the silence, she told him about Arthur's call and his anxieties. "It could be possible. Everyone came to Charles because he was good since he isn't around anymore the downfall is expected. This time, we had to be there but you choose to be here." "What do you think? Should I approach Mr. Smith about the order?" "You never bothered to tell me about your business lunch. Why are you asking now?" "It was a business lunch that is all." "I just do not want you to be hurt. Please keep strictly to business. Call Arthur and let him follow up with Mr. Smith. You deal with your pots only. Am I clear?" "Crystal clear," Chloe was quick to respond.

"What's up, Bro? Are you wide awake?" Asked Chloe as they walked into the drawing room of her house. Since they would be late Clove and Chloe had dinner in the hospital cafeteria. Uncle Connor and Clove played along while having dinner. Camila was laughing looking at the banter, they were scolded to maintain silence by the nurses. Chloe had a chicken burger she wasn't very hungry but she was surprised to see her brother up this late. "I was preoccupied with something," he replied

"Did you and Dad fight again?" "Why do you think so?" "Well, I can read you like a book. That face you make resembles a cow when you ruminate on his thoughts." Now Chloe was ruminating before James. "Everything does not need to be Dad-centric." Lashing his anger at her James got up and just walked out.

Chloe was taken aback; she never thought her brother was so sensitive. After all the time spent together, never had he turned his back on her. "Madam, would you be requiring anything?" The butler asked Chloe. That got her back to her senses "Could I get a cup of coffee up in my room?" Asked Chloe, she had to be awake as she would be working late in the night on the designs for Mr. Smith. "Of course, I will bring it myself." replied the butler. "Madam, don't mind Master James. The poor soul didn't mean to hurt you. Today is Ms. Emma's death anniversary. Master James asked Sir to keep a prayer service in her memory. Which was declined; as she died by suicide, and you know how stubborn Sir Raven can get at times." The butler was interrupted by Chloe asking him, "Emma and suicide? Why did she?" "I thought you knew." "I did not! Would you tell me more about this?" requested Chloe. "Madam, Ms. Emma was in love with Mr. Philip Smith. You met him at your welcome party. Our master and his father agreed upon their marriage. Philip would be given a handsome dowry and his own construction company. But Mr. Philip was away; clueless about these plans. He was in love with another woman. So, his Dad withdrew the deal as his son's happiness mattered the most. Mr. Raven broke, the news to Ms. Emma. Initially, nobody noticed that she was unhappy with the change of events. Brother James was the only one counseling her late in the night, he had not joined the priesthood. She had taken a vow from him to remain silent. Meanwhile, Mr. Raven found another match for Ms. Emma. He was Mr. Michael he was a warm and well-behaved boy. I liked him. They were engaged but Mr. Philip attended the party with his wife. That night Ms. Emma drank a lot of wine drowning in the swimming pool in the backyard. Sir told people that she was diagnosed with ovarian cancer, and the pain was driving her crazy. She felt unconscious and fell in the pool resulting in her death. But I know she drowned herself to death. She was unhappy. Sir was the first to find her in the pool. After her death, brother James became an introvert, drawn from all at home. He started being in the company of Pastor Ben. His life changed, the Lord touched him and he has gone to serve the people through his vocation." "Thank you. A lot has happened since I wasn't around. Now I would like to go up. Never mind. Don't bother with the coffee. I don't feel like it." 'My God!' her father had lied to her. His flesh and blood. She was feeling numb after hearing Emma's story. How could she die? Her baby sister was silently suffering and she was unaware, living her life. The whole thought was nauseous. She couldn't work any further. She called it a day, retiring to bed.

Chapter 12

Work, Work, and More Work

"Well, I liked the miniature table pots in the figurine form with flower arrangements, the color on the pots with our logo color combination, is appreciated and the huge pots for the welcome area too, but can you give a candle stand or holder to be placed on the windows? I want to give it an earthy and pastel appearance. I want fragrant candles to be lit." Mr. Philip Smith was looking at the designs presented before him, discussing them with Chloe. "How would you like incense burners?" "No, I want scented candles. I like the fragrance," "Would you mind if we create animal forms with floating candles?" "Can you show me samples for the same? I am finding it difficult to picture." "Oh! I will ask Arthur to bring along the samples from the manufactory. Another thing, my husband had met you with Connor for the uniform upgrade, did someone get it? Are you open for discussions?" "To be very frank that isn't my domain and interest, dad wanted to change. I did not, so we have a difference of opinion. Let me check with him if he is free and maybe we will go through it tomorrow." "Can Arthur meet you both to look into this matter?" "Are you, busy tomorrow? Shall we postpone it?" Mr. Smith raised his eyebrows looking at her for some clarity. "No, I am not." "Then I think that settles it. Let us have an informal meeting at my place. Dad will be around, let us discuss this over lunch?" Mr. Philip was looking at her with those puppy eyes that melted Chloe's reservations and she agreed to the plan.

Chloe called Arthur filling him in on the progress and instructed him to do what was required she asked him to send her the file and meet her in person. As Chloe walked to her car she was feeling happy, strong, and confident. She felt as if she had lived her life in the shadow of her husband. Today she felt something equivalent to climbing Mount Everest. As she drove towards her home she had a smile on her face and was looking forward to lunch with them.

As she entered home her mother greeted her. Clove had gone out with James to a water park. Chloe took this opportunity to ask her mother about Emma. "Mother, can I trust you to tell me the truth about Emma? Every time, I get different versions. At least you can give her a true tribute by telling me what happened?" Chloe had tears trickling down her eyes, her mother was shocked turning around to ask her, "What have you heard so far?" "It is not important what I have heard. What is important is what happened in reality?" Chloe was coaxing her mother and she knew that she would let her know. "Your Dad felt cheated when you betrayed us and walked away with Charles. I do not know if you remember but Philip studied with you in college but in a different section. Dad had the contract to construct the chain of hotels for Mr. Smith. Dad began to like him and wanted to get you married to him. But he wanted to pursue his career and went to do hotel management abroad. Meanwhile, Dad pinned his hopes on Emma to get her married to Philip when you were out of the scene. Mr. Smith was convinced by the business proposal and accepted Emma. Emma slowly started having feelings for him. When he returned he fell for his head chef and finally, the marriage proposal was called off. Emma was left shattered. We found the next best match we could. Mr. Henry's son Michael. I loved his warm nature. He would cheer her up. She started to open up to him. On the engagement, Philip landed with his wife. Emma couldn't bear to see him happy. She felt humiliated by him publicly, she was so angry that she ended up drinking a lot of wine. After the party ended Michael took her near the pool, they ended up fighting so he walked away while she stayed. Your father saw her fall in the pool from the window in our room. He rushed to save her but she drowned. The only mistake your father made then, as he was going through a financial crunch was to use her death to get insurance coverage. He proved that she had ovarian cancer and forged the truth. James was hurt, and prayers were his only consolation That is when God spoke to him and he found his vocation, his path to healing. Both of them are not on the best of terms but yes, the love is not lost." Mrs. Rebecca continued, "Dad has been very happy and chirpy since you came. He loves spending time with Clove. James sees Emma in her. Everyone is now seeing a ray of hope through Clove. Please don't take it away from us, we will die." Mrs. Rebecca was crying out loud. Chloe hugged her to console her. She told her, she wasn't going anywhere, she was here to stay. Mrs. Rebecca was relieved, hugging her back. She was so happy to hear her. Rebecca was also happy to know that the pottery orders were confirmed.

Chloe went to her bedroom. She had been busy since morning, so she called Connor. Connor filled her in on the treatment plan, he was happy to know that her designs were liked and upset about the upcoming lunch. She promised to send Clove as well to meet them in the evening. Connor asked her not to bother with the hospital visit as he knew she was settling in. Chloe was caught up with so much happening around her. 'Tomorrow is a big day' she thought to herself. She had her bath and rest, as she had been up all night drawing the designs.

Chloe was beginning to like Mr. Smith; she was drawn to him. He had an aura around him which was strong she didn't understand why she was letting another man in her life. Charles was not in person, she missed his hugs so much. She felt guilty of thinking that she was getting on in life without him.

She argued with herself in her mind while lying in the bathtub. The phone rang it, was Camilla Chloe was worried she was hoping for some good news. "Hello! Hi there! How are you feeling? All good?" "I guess you have forgotten us. Only Clove religiously came to meet me." Chole interrupted. "I know I have been bad and I apologize, is there a chance I can make it up to you?" "Get your ass here for dinner because I am making shepherd's pie. I feel like cooking after a long time. Connor doesn't want to eat anymore. I do not feel like eating anymore as I vomit more. The least I want is to spend time with you." "I will be there. I don't think you would fancy me in my birthday suit." To which Camila laughed. "I will be waiting."

Chloe rang the doorbell. She had got Camila's favorite, wine and cheese. She was dressed in her green dress with frills. She was hoping, she would love it. "I was planning on filing a missing complaint you made it just in time," Camila said being sarcastic. Chloe was speechless. Camila had lost weight, was bald, and looked pale. Connor did tell her about the surgery and chemotherapy sessions but she could not picture that it would turn out to be so bad. Chloe took a minute to compose herself, she did not want her friend to read her thoughts out aloud, "I am guilty madam, all yours." Chloe wanted to go with the flow. "Chloe, it is so good to see you." Camila hugged her. "Where's Connor?" "He has gotten busy. Shuttling between factory and outlets. He comes home and crashes on the bed. There are these nights where I vomit or I have ulcers and all the burning. I feel suicidal. I cannot take it anymore." Camila was in tears. "I was not a good wife. I could not give him a baby. I know, but he never says anything. He has always been good, my pillar of strength. Chloe, can I ask you something?" To which she nodded. Camila continued, "If things take a wrong turn, I lose my life fighting this disease will you care for Connor?" "Nothing is going to happen. Nobody is going anywhere." Chloe assured, but Camila was not satisfied. She pestered her. Finally, Chloe gave in and said yes.

Camila had a smile that looked peaceful. Chloe was not sure why she acted so. She had known Camila for a long time, never for once she was weak. All their lives were twisted, they had to hang in there.

"Camilla, there is something I want you to know?" Chloe, was shy when she said so. "What is it?" Camila inquired. "I kind of like Mr. Philip my business partner, but I am guilty at the same time as Charles has always been the love of my life, I feel torn apart. I am so confused am I ready to move on? Or is this a fancy?" perplexed Chloe blurted out her fears. She was afraid that this friendship which was blooming should not take a turn where she would regret her decision. After Emma's suicide, it had complicated matters more so for her.

Camila spoke up to give her advice, "Chloe! My mother always told me, If you love someone for their looks it is obsession, if you love someone for their kindness it is admiration, if you love someone for money then it is interest, if you love someone because they love you then it is empathy, if you love someone despite their flaws then it is true acceptance, if you love someone though thick and thin then it is genuine commitment, if you love someone for their mind and intellect it is intellectual attraction, if you love someone deeply even when you are apart it is, an emotional connection, if you love someone and prioritize their happiness over your own it is selflessness, if you love someone for the way they make you laugh it is humor based affection, if you love someone for the shared experiences and memories it is nostalgia driven love, you love someone unconditionally flaws and all it is pure unconditional love, if you are confused why you love this person then it is definitely love and then do not let it go, cling on to that man, if you think it is Philip, then nothing is too soon."

Chloe thanked Camila for now she had her answer, it was admiration for his character and nothing more. They watched their favorite movie dinner, and wine; laughed at old memories. It was great for both of them. It was late, Connor was not there yet but she had to leave so she thanked Camilla and left.

Chapter 13

The First Kiss

Chloe was in a chauffeur-driven car. Mr. Smith had it sent for her. It was the first time she was visiting his house as she crossed the main gate, she saw acres of parkland. As they were approaching the house she saw railed paddocks, a portico with windows, and plenty of attic space probably for their servants unlike theirs where the servants lived in their quarters; the big house was elegant with Italian plasterwork and fine timber probably acquired from the colonies. The doors and floors were probably carved out of Baltic pine. She was amazed to see such grandeur. No wonder, they had such good taste.

The butler was very welcoming, he took her coat from her and ushered her in. The drawing room was huge and decorated with trophies and animal mounts. She could see deer mounts, bear mounts, and tiger mounts, a bear rug on the floor; porcelain from the east, a rhino foot ashtray. Chloe was a little shocked to see the paper cutting of hunting and Asian people looking over the dead animal framed. She stopped to read it when she sensed someone standing behind her, it was Philip. He had worn a green T-shirt and beige cotton pants. His perfume gave away his presence, Chloe loved the fragrance. They both greeted each other. Chloe was in black jeans and a pink T-shirt. She had worn her hair in a bun along with dangling earrings. The pink matt lipstick went well.

"Welcome home, dear." Mr. Smith Senior said and continued, "I have heard so much about you that I couldn't wait to meet you." Chloe replied, "The feeling is mutual." Mr. Philip said, "Let's sit down here would you like to go to the dining area?" "I would prefer the dining area I am a little uncomfortable with the mounts." Mr. Smith intervened pointing towards Philip getting Chloe's attention. He laughingly said, "They are the trophies of great memories of my grandfathers, father, and myself on hunting. Those were the days when all the glory was. This chicken has nothing to do with it." "Come on Dad, let us move on." Saying this Mr. Philip escorted all of them towards the dining room. The dining room had portraits of the ladies of the house. It was so unfortunate that this house had none of them alive.

"I wanted to know if it is okay to discuss work." Asked Chloe "No dear, no work today. It has been ages since we have entertained people here. He just works and I am unable to entertain as I am bound to this chair." Said Mr. Smith Senior. There was sadness in his eyes. Chloe thought in her mind how difficult it would be to be bound to a chair. Mr. Smith was a thin, tall, and slender individual. He was fair with sparse black hair. He had black eyes and his face had begun showing wrinkles. He wore a smile at all times but the sadness in his eyes spoke volumes.

There was food, chatter, laughter, and a sense of past grandeur. Mr. Smith spoke about all the countries he traveled to for work, the places, and the cultures he had experienced. He had kept a diary for each country. He asked the butler to fetch him one as Chloe went through it. Chloe was struck with the idea, "Why don't you publish this work as a travelogue? All you need to do is elaborate about the place and your travel experience" "I have no experience in writing." "If you could write all this, I think it is a start. All you need to do is give it a human touch." Saying this she smiled, Philip intervened and said, "Yes! Where there is a will there is a way, Dad."

Mr. Smith Senior looked pleased and excited as if he had found a new way to keep himself occupied, excused himself after a while, and left them to retire to his room. "Would you like a walk or tour of the house?" Asked Philip. "Yes, I would love the walk," said Chloe. So, they got off the table and went outside the house. Philip had a small lake where he bred fish and loved fishing in his spare time. After he lost his wife to the accident he spent his time there. It gave him the much-needed quiet to think. He wanted to show Chloe the spot as she took him to hers. "This is my favorite spot. I hate being indoors, even as a kid. My father made this lake as my mom loved to eat fish. She loved to eat freshwater fish." Said Philip with a smile. "My mom tells me that we went to college together. I don't remember seeing you." "Yes, in a way. I was there for only three months. We lost Mom and Dad pulled me out of college and I went to another one. Life those days were tough; I was going through a rough patch." Philip continued, "There is something I want to clear the air about. If is okay to talk. It is about Emma." "I too wanted to hear your version," Chloe replied. "There is nothing like my version. People think that I am to be blamed. I didn't know that Dad chose her. Even if I married her, I would have never been able to keep her happy. I loved my wife, I was madly in love with her. I could not think of a life without her. I am sorry what happened to Emma but I wanted you to know it was one-sided." Philip felt good after stating his side of the story. "Of late, in a long time, I have developed feelings for someone. I am afraid to say it aloud." "That is a good thing. Very few people have a second chance in life. I think you should take it no matter what." Chloe reassured him.

"Chloe, I want to tell you that I feel a very strong attraction towards you. Everything about you makes me weak. I like the way you look at me. I like the way you smile. I want to be your shoulder to cry on. Allow me to care, love, and nurture you. Let us walk holding hands in hands. Let us be there for each other. We both have lost our loved ones. Let us put the pain behind us. Clove, you, and me. Let us start afresh." Saying this Philip kissed Chloe on her cheeks. He was holding her hands gently as he got down on one knee. Before he could ask the question, they were interrupted by Connor. Chloe was in shock when she pulled away, excusing herself from Philip. "Hello!" Connor interrupted her, he sounded distressed, "I need you please come, it's Camilla. She has tried suicide. She slit her wrist. I found her in a pool of blood. She has lost a lot of blood, she is sinking I need you, just come" "I will be there as soon as I can." Saying this she hung up. She informed Philip who wanted to accompany her. He knew they held a special place in her heart and since he knew Connor, he felt sorry for him. Chloe was adamant that she wanted to go alone. He arranged for his driver to drop her to the hospital.

"Connor, how is Camilla? What happened?" Chloe was shaking. Connor who was lost in thought, held onto a paper. All he did was raise his head and he had a blank expression. He passed the paper onto Chloe. She started to read the paper. The paper was Camilla's suicide note. Camila wrote to Connor –

My Dear Husband,

Life has been kind to me. Together we built each brick of our house and business. We had our hardships and our joys. We had friends who became our family. We almost forgot our family members. We had Clove, even if we didn't have our own.

But today as I look back I feel a gloom upon me. I feel like a loser. I was okay when we had nothing, I was okay when we could not have our baby, and I was okay with us shifting to the city with uncertainty, but I am not okay fighting for my life.

Maybe when you get this letter. I will leave you. I know I have disappointed you, left you early, and given up on life, but I really can't go on like this. I hope you understand that I took my life for I couldn't continue it on bits and pieces, begging for it.

I am entrusting your care with Chloe. I know you may not want her to. But she promised me to take care of you. Clove will be your strength. Cling on to your newfound family and be the light as you were mine.

I want you to know I loved you always and I know you loved me too. But, live your life to the fullest and be safe and happy always.

Your loving wife,

Camila

PS: Please bury me in the town cemetery. Because those were the happy days of my life and I would want to rest there forever. Nobody cries at my funeral. I want smiling faces. Send me with a smile. I do not want crowds.

After Chloe read the note she sat next to Connor. There was pin-drop silence between them. Chloe was the first one to break the silence, "I did not know that she would give up on life. She was sounding different and odd. Still, this is shocking," Connor was speechless. So was Chloe.

In the meanwhile, Chloe's phone rang. She did not answer. It was Philip her head was clouded. She needed some time away from him the least.

Connor called Pastor Tony, informing him. He was willing to do what was necessary. Connor was calm, in thought, and composed. Chloe asked Connor, "Will you share your pain with me or not?" "What pain are you talking about? Everyone gets to decide for themselves except me, Charles who made his decision. Camila, she took her decisions and only I had to follow and accept them. How selfish she was to take her life. She also wants you to follow her decisions"

Dr. Mark approached them and said, "Mr. Connor I am sorry. We lost Mrs. Camila, but we did our best. I will try to release the body as early as I can." Chloe was devastated, as she was clinging to hope for a miracle. Tears were silently flowing from their eyes. Chloe reached out to Connor and hugged him.

They stood there comforting each other like in the old times. Connor was deeply hurt at what Camila had done. But nothing could be done now, it was too late.

Chapter 14

Missing

Connor honored Camila's last wish. Her parents were dead, and she had an elder sister's family who made it to the funeral. On his side, he had lost both his parents, but his brother's family made it to the funeral. It was a close family farewell. Camila was loved and honored, they played her favorite songs and all fought their tears including Clove. She was brave, she wrote her a letter, placing it over her grave. She was disappointed that she was not able to spend time with her during her last few hours on Earth.

Today was the ninth-day prayer meeting. Prayers were said, and music was being played. Her favorite food was served. All her friends and family were there. Mr. Philip made his presence felt. All their workers were there. The meeting was held at Chloe's house. They had put up a portrait of Camila next to Charles. Her smiling face welcomed everyone like old times. Everyone missed her warm hugs. She was a good soul, but it was too soon to see her go.

It had started getting late, the guests had started to leave. Chloe and Connor were seeing off all the guests. Clove sat silently on the couch. Camila's death had brought back painful memories for her, coming back here was even more painful. To be with her grandparents had done her good, all the love and attention helped her deal with her pain. She did not want to lose more people.

"Philip, may I have a word with you?" Chloe requested his company as she led him away from Connor over to the corner of the room and lowered her voice to whisper, "Philip, I am very sorry about the other day." She was interrupted by Philip "I am sorry that I kissed you as I realized you were not ready, I get it, I know you are very close to them and hearing about Camilla would have broken your heart, I know you wanted to rush and needed the privacy, but I want you to know that I have taken a liking for you and I want to marry you, as I haven't felt this comfortable in years with anyone other than you. Loneliness was my only companion you appeared like hope and your arrival changed everything without trying, you brought me peace the kind that soothes the soul, and slowly you became the one I needed. I think I got everything in you I was wishing for, you reminded me of what my mother said that the best things in life came when you never anticipated it, So I wanted to give us a try. But if you are not ready I understand."

Chloe replied, "Thank you for loving me, when I needed company, you are genuinely a sweet soul, as you make me feel safe, the time spent together in a way is helping me heal my pain, I am glad I met you, and it feels like I know you longer than I know you, and I truly enjoyed every moment with you, but I now understand that I admire not love you. I am sorry I cannot marry you, but in you I see a good friend I have lost one I want to make another, Emma will always be between us, I cannot forget that she loved you. I am sorry I cannot marry you but I can assure you I can be the best of friends."

Philip although disappointed had tears in his eyes and smiled saying, "I would love that. Now you need to excuse me, I have to head back to the city as tomorrow your dad and I would be heading out early to acquire some lands for our next joint venture. See you soon."

Chloe walked him towards the door and waved goodbye as he drove his car out the driveway.

It was time for bed. Connor retired to the guest room, Clove and Chloe went to their bedrooms to sleep. Clove was unable to sleep alone so she went to her mother's room. Her mother lay on the bed, awake. Clove entered the room and asked her mother if she could share the bed with her. Chloe was more than happy and she moved to her side waiting for her to hop in. Clove spoke first," Mumma can we speak before we doze off?". "Yes, sweetheart. What is it you want to talk about?" Clove continued, "Isn't it weird? I feel bad, one by one all those I love are leaving me. I am scared mummy, I don't want to lose Uncle Connor or you." Chloe hugged her tightly. "Do not worry sweetheart, we are not going anywhere. I want to see you grow to be a fine woman, have a boyfriend, fall in love, have kids and do well in your career." Clove responded," Mummy, we have lots of time for this, I have my examinations next month. Mummy, did you like someone before Dad?" Chloe was smiling, "Actually, yes. Before I got to know your dad I briefly dated Uncle Connor. Maybe two months, but we both felt like we were meant to be good friends then your dad came along and Uncle Connor got Aunty Camila, we remained great friends till date." "Mummy what will happen to Uncle Connor now? Will he live with us or alone?" "Sweetheart, I haven't asked him, he needs some time alone, let it be his choice and his decision to do what he wants. Let us give him time to make his decision." "Mummy, I heard Uncle Philip speaking with you, he was talking as if you were upset with him after the kiss and why were you not answering his phone? Are you in love with him?" Chloe reached out for the night lamp. She sat up and looked into Clove's eyes and spoke, "Baby, when you are an adult, things do get complicated. Yes, Uncle Philip kissed me on my cheeks, but I was not ready, I like him as a person or a friend but I don't love him." "Do you love Uncle Connor? Can you marry him? I want him to be with us, not Uncle Philip. Please mummy?" Chloe just hugged her for the time being. She had no answers. Chloe said, "Let us sleep for now. I love you darling, please remember this, nobody is more important than you." Clove though never got a clear reply but slept off, but Chloe was restless the whole night. She was thinking all about what Clove had said, what Philip had asked, and what she had promised Camila.

Chloe came down the stairs and wished Connor good morning. She had slept late in the wee hours and so woke up late. Connor asked Chloe, "All good? Why is Clove not down for breakfast?" A surprised Chloe answered, "When I woke up I did not see her in the room. I thought she was with you. I do not think she is upstairs. You check with the neighbors, while I search the house." They split. There was no sign of Clove. Chloe was in a panic while, Connor called the school to check if she was there. But every place they could think of did not give them their desired answer. It was as if she had vanished. They thought it to wait a few hours before they could report. Soon the news spread far. Pastor Tony came to their house. He informed them that the filling station worker on the outskirts of the town saw Clove riding her bicycle towards the city somewhere at 5 a.m. But his shift changed at 6 am and he did not know if she returned. Chloe and Connor were wondering why would she want to go that road. They both decided to hit the road to check on her. Meanwhile, Pastor Tony told them that he would inform them if she returned here. They thanked him, sat in the car, and drove off towards the highway.

Connor asked Chloe, "Do you have any idea what this is all about? Chloe then filled him in on the previous night's talk that she had with Clove. Connor confessed,

"This is not the first time that she has brought this up. She briefly asked me a day before she asked you. But I didn't think that she was this serious." "What was your reply?" "I told her I cannot stop loving her even if I do not marry your mother. If you feel that marrying her proves it. Then I will, But not now. I need to reconcile my pain. Chloe, I think I want to call it quits on the city life. I want to sell off everything except the house. Since Camila is not there, I don't want to go to the factory and the Bakery anymore. I don't know what I will do. But I will buy a house here and clear my head." Chloe looked at him and said, "You can have your house, but I assure you, you can stay with us as long as you want." "I can, but there will be a time when we may not want it, or people who we love and respect us may not want us living together. But that is a later thing. My priority is to find Clove and sort out this mess." "Philip loves me, Connor. He proposed to me. But I did not give him a reply he needed." Hearing this Connor stopped his vehicle, "When did this happen?" "The day Camila died, I was with him." "What was your reply?" Chloe looked at Connor and said, "The man I love is no more. But there is someone who I can spend the rest of my life knowing will care for me and love my daughter. I look up to him and I have always and will always." Connor bowed his head saying, "Philip will be a lucky man." Chloe went closer to Connor and gave him a peck on the cheeks. "He never stood a chance before you. We are here because destiny put us together, I think of it now how we found our way to each other despite so many people, you are on my mind, and now a part of my breath, in my soul, I can't envision the remaining of my life without you, we both lived through a lot till we found our way back when I saw you for the first time I felt an overwhelming sense of rightness, I now see clarity like all the stars have aligned for us everything happens for a reason, I believe we were meant to find each other and that makes our bond special and that is what sustains us, I wouldn't trade this for anything, we had other people in our lives just to lead us back to each other."

Connor had tears running down his cheeks, they were hugging each other. Life had been hard for both of them. They had stood the test of time. This was like a ray of hope. They had known each other and above all, Clove was comfortable with both and after all of this, she would be happy to know that her wish was being fulfilled.

Connor kissed her hand and drove further until they reached a crossroad and were choosing which one would they take. They were confident as they were in this together this time. It would be a matter of time before Clove would be with them. They were excited to just see the smile on Cloves' face their decision would bring. If only, she had never acted rashly and waited a little longer.

So, they took the road to the city hoping she would want to go to her grandparents, hoping to catch up with her.

Chapter 15

Uninvited

"Ah! My head and leg hurt, cannot move. Where am I?" Clove was surrounded by darkness. She had gotten up early; seeing her mother asleep she decided to go for a bicycle ride. She thought some exercise would do her good. The time was perfect as there would be less traffic.

The plan was to cycle to the outskirts and come back. But before she could make a turn she saw her grandfather sitting with Mr. Philip Smith in his car. They were headed towards the city. She tried to get their attention while riding her bicycle. She wanted to know why they were there so early and why they were not coming over. She tried her best to follow them but at the crossroad, she did not see the truck coming from the opposite side, in a split second she moved backwards, slipped and fell down the cliff as she was at the edge. This saved her life, but as she tumbled down the steep edges, she was bruised by all the shrubs and rocks with which she came in contact. Her leg got stuck in a shrub and she felt a sharp pain causing her to pass out. As she rolled down the edge it was steeper, she fell inside a groove carved at the bottom of a Haworth Tree that was there.

She was in that pit for four long hours, lying unconscious. She tried hard to move once she had regained consciousness. She was hungry, tired, bleeding, and weak. She looked at her right leg, it was swollen. She understood that she had broken her leg and that made her incapacitate to move as every little move would make her wince. She was not willing to die in this pit. She wished for a fairy godmother to appear as it had been before for Cinderella. With the light entering through the opening she could say that it was afternoon; the sun shone brightly and it felt warm. As the sun's rays entered the room through the opening, she could see vaguely inside the pit. There was a small bed with a side table far from where she was, a toadstool and a small table with a candle stick, small utensils and a small earthen brick place with firewood alongside. To one end of the room, she saw green and red suits with matching crooked hats. She saw a sword and wands. Where was she? She knew about fairies. Was she in one's house? Why the suits and swords? Was she in a dwarf's house? Fear gripped her. She was uncertain of the outcome of the meeting but this was her only chance to meet her mother. Either way, she would die or ask for help to be reunited.

The chain of thoughts was broken when she heard laughter and two people's footsteps approaching her pit could it be help? Or was the horror to unfold? Time will only tell.

Chloe and Connor were scanning the way to the city. There were no accidents and above all, there was no sign of Clove. They pulled over for some tea at the filling station. Chloe called her mom, "Mom, is Clove there by any chance?" "No Honey, is everything all right? Is Clove missing? Dad and Mr. Philip had a business meeting in the wee hours and they were in the nearby village to acquire some land for work they would be on their way; I will page him." "No, I will, do not bother, she would be with him. We had a difference of opinion, she left home on her bicycle, and maybe Dad would have spotted her." "Good Heavens! Dad will take care of it. We will send a search party. Where are you?" "I am on my way, coming over with Connor." While they were conversing, Chloe's

Dad was back home, he assured Chloe that he would take the necessary steps for Clove as she was dear to him. He was composed and he made the necessary phone calls, the police sprang into action. He sent his staff to scan every area surrounding the radius of twelve kilometers from the town where they were residing. "You scan the skies if necessary, I want my granddaughter back safe and sound." That was his order. So, Chloe and Connor proceeded to go to the city to be with Chloe's family.

Clove could sense the footsteps loud and clear whoever it was they were nearby; she could hear them speak. "Who could have discovered your house, mate?" The first one spoke to the other. "I have no clue, I had the opening all covered." The second person replied. "Let's get our wands out because I have left my sword in." "Could it be from the mundane world (non-magic folk) or ours?" Asked the first one. "I wasn't expecting anyone though so we partied today," The second one said. "Stay alert, on the count of three," said the first. "Blaze!" Shouting this magical word, the two little men entered the pit and the entire pit was lit. Clove was blinded by the light. When she could finally open her eyes, she saw two little men with wrinkled faces and long beards approximately about three feet high and one dressed in a little red jacket, with red breeches buckled at the knee, black stockings, and a hat, cocked in the style while the other in the same attire but in green. The entire pit was lit with the light emerging from the wand. She could now see better that this could be one of these little men's house.

"Restrain," the red-dressed man said. Immediately the vines started to tie Clove's hands and feet together. The green-dressed man walked towards Clove, caught her by her hair, and angrily asked, "Who are you? Why are you here? Speak up." Clove fearfully spoke, "I am

Clove, I mean no harm, I fell from the cliff and tumbled down. I broke my leg and I am unable to move. I want to go home. Please help me. My cycle would be near the road you can check for it." The green-clothed man looked in the direction of the red-clothed man who snapped his fingers, "Flee." In split seconds he disappeared, and before Clove could take the next breath he reappeared this time sitting on her broken cycle. This was clear to Clove that they were fairies or maybe something like fairies but would they be kind was what was racing in her mind.

Both the men went to the side and started to speak occasionally glancing at Clove. The red-clothed man said, "She is telling the truth mate, I found her cycle broken at the beginning of the cliff and as I came down I saw pieces of her dress along the shrubs and bushes. She is mundane and we are safe, Emerald" "Apple, what if she is here for my gold?" asked Emerald. "No, only if you reveal to have, she is a child I don't think she knows we are leprechauns," replied Apple. "What do we do now? How do we get rid of her?" asked Emerald. "She is a child we cannot kill her but we can erase her memory, mending her fracture magically will take twelve hours, we can mend her bone, teleport her to her house, and then, erase her memory. I will get wine for her from the cellar to numb her senses," saying this Apple disappeared.

"Please don't kill me," Clove begged Emerald. "Nonsense, I won't," replied Emerald. He pulled the toadstool and sat, facing Clove. "I am a little hungry. I haven't eaten anything since morning. Could I get something to eat and drink? Anything would be fine." She was pleading as her stomach growled. "Very well" Emerald snapped his fingers and before Clove appeared a plate of potatoes and chicken roast. Clove looked pleadingly to untie her hands, but the contents of the plate arose; a single potato flew towards her mouth and when she opened it to take a bite, it vanished. Emerald fell off his toadstool laughing. Hungry and disappointed Clove began to cry. "Did you think I would serve you food? I am free, not anyone's slave, I do as I please." "I have never seen people like you before, who are you? Are you fairies?" Clove was interested to know who she had stumbled upon in her distress. "I am Emerald; the Leprechaun not like you mundane." He proudly said with an air of superiority. "What does mundane mean?" asked Clove. "Mundane means you, non-magic folk," replied Emerald. "You do magic. I don't think so. It failed terribly as the food you served vanished," Clove mocked trying to instigate him to serve her food. "My folks are known to play mischief on you, mundane," By saying this Emerald showed no signs of budging.

"See I have a broken leg, I mean no harm, the least you could give me is a glass of water." Clove was bargaining for something to have. "Very well I have dandelion tea. If it suits you." Emerald softened a little. "Yes please." Clove was willing to drink poison to moisten her throat. Emerald brought her the tea which was piping hot. He used his wand to untie her hand and gave her the tea to have. With the first sip, she spat out the tea that she had sipped in. "What do you want apple juice now?" an angry Emerald asked her. "I am sorry; it was boiling. I burned my mouth. Can I have a glass of water?" asked Clove. The taste was so strong that Clove could not drink it. She was hoping just for a glass of water. Emerald snapped his fingers and the pitcher with water and an empty glass landed in front of Clove. Clove poured herself a glass of water from the pitcher. The water was cold and Clove drank two glasses full. Her thirst was quenched. But she needed to quieten her growling stomach. She thanked him and asked, "When will your parents come? How old are you?" Emerald raised his eyebrows in wonder, "My parents, how old do you think I am?" "Well, judging that you cannot cook, you could be…" she was interrupted by Emerald, "I cannot cook, just wait, I can make a nice stir fry mushroom stew with freshly found roots." Saying this he headed toward the direction of the earthen brick place, he snapped his fingers and Clove saw the vegetables being cut by the knife, the pot being placed on the fire and the ingredients tossed in one by one until the aroma of the stew filled the entire place. Emerald bought the mushroom stew in a bowl and served it before her. Clove took a sip, her eyes widened, and the stew was so delicious that she licked the bowl dry. She thanked Emerald for the stew, she was sleepy now and instantaneously dozed off to sleep.

Chapter 16

The Bond

"No, we stick to the original plan." Emerald had blurted these words so loudly that he woke Clove, who was fast asleep. Apple had arrived and they disagreed on something but Clove was unclear about what it might be.

"There you are wide awake, time to grow and mend your bones, here is a decoction of Arnica, Ruta, and Symphytum and I am sure it should do you good. Provided you drink off it every hour for the next twelve hours. I must warn you it has a bitter taste." Saying this, Apple stuffed the decoction which was in a small measuring cup into Clove's hand. "OK mate, I have to leave. My work here is done, the coast is clear, I will come at dawn. I have put protective enchantments around the house to make it difficult to spot." Apple shook his head and apparated.

"Is he your brother?" Clove asked Emerald. "We don't usually have siblings. He is a friend." Emerald was tight-lipped. "Oh! That is just sad. I too have no siblings. I miss having a brother or a sister. But I have lovely parents. Correction parent. I lost my dad and my aunt all in this year." Saying this, tears rolled down as she continued, "Can you bring back the dead with your magic?" "Of course not, why would you want to do that, we mend shoes and regenerate bones. That's why we are mending your bones. Now drink it, if you want to walk on your legs" He ordered her.

Clove unwillingly drank it. She grimaced; it was bitter. "What were you expecting? Fruit juices?" He raised his wand, and said, "Instead with a face like that you would look good as a pig. *Metamorphose!*" Clove's head turned into a pig. She began to growl. "Very well, Veto!" Saying this he transfigured her back to her original self. "Thank you I love my face." an irritated Clove spoke.

Emerald went to his workstation where he began mending shoes. "What do you do all day?" asked Clove. "None of your business," he replied in a rude tone. "Well! We are stuck with each other. So, let's get to know each other." "Young lady, I love it when it is quiet, I am used to solitude, and I do not acknowledge your presence. My details are off your limits. Now let me work," saying this, he went back to mending his shoes. Clove was used to the attention since she was not getting any from him, so she started to hum. "What is with the humming? Keep it down," ordered Emerald. "Give me something to do I am bored. My dad used to give me some work when he was working. It used to be fun. You know he stitched lovely suits." Clove was remembering the fun times with her father. She continued, "Do you have memories of your childhood?" "All people do not have a great childhood." Emerald was rude and ignored her altogether. "Ah! I see. You know, Mother says sharing sorrows multiplies happiness." Clove was persistent almost nagging.

The clock in the room struck to the next hour. Emerald snapped his fingers once again. The decoction was magically poured and appeared before Clove. Clove was careful this time. She just gulped down the decoction without a single word. "A fast learner. You deserve a treat," saying so he magically sent fruits in a bowl towards her. The bowl had strawberries, bananas, and oranges. Clove took a handful of strawberries, a banana, and an orange. She was happily eating fruits. "Hmm! You like to eat or are you hungry?" Emerald had started to soften. After all, she was just a child. "I love to eat. I had great cooks, my aunt had a bakery." Her face lit up remembering all the goodies she used to eat.

"Tell me something about you, will you? You are all touch me and I will kill you." Clove was curious to know about him. "Back at home, I have read all princess stories with magic, please tell me something at least," she begged.

Emerald stopped his mending and for the first time, he looked at her. All this while he was talking with his head down, mending the heap of shoes he sat next to. He said, "You have my mother's eyes. My mother was a fallen fairy as I am told, she was Fairy Queen mother Titania's, younger sister Mab, she came to our Kingdom of the Sky to spend time with our queen. Our island is the most beautiful fairy island. King Oberon was a kind and benevolent ruler. His rule is still known as the golden era. There was a truce made by the Gods so that all magical folk would live in peace and harmony. Each magical kind ruled over their part of the kingdom.

Princess Mab went for a stroll in the evenings along the sea coast. She once saw a ship wreckage on the shore, a human, or mundane as we say was discovered. He was very handsome. Princess Mab fell in love with him. King Oberon was upset as never a mundane was permitted into our island. But when Princess Mab requested, he obliged. He survived and thanked us. Since he was married and had a family on the land, he was grateful but never responded to the warm affection of Princess Mab during his healing. This enraged her and she magically erased his family's memory. They were wed in a grand three-day celebration against our King and Queen's wishes. But he was always aloof as if he didn't belong there. One day he accidentally discovered his past life. People who lived to tell the tale say that he was filled with vengeance, he took his life saying that she had his body but not his soul, it was too late the damage was done. My mother had conceived me. He tormented her every night till I was born. The fairies out of fear hid me from him on the mainland. My mother was taken away with his spirit as she was stripped of a fairy status for she married him. We do not know what happened to her. Her belongings like the wand, her cloak, and her dagger are still preserved in a trunk." He had a painful expression even though he fought his tears well yet, his eyes spoke tales of the sorrowful past.

Clove was moved by his pain. In the third hour, she took the third dose and her pain disappeared, but her legs felt weak she still, could not move them. Seeing this Emerald said, "Don't move that leg, the healing has just started. With the next dose, you will be able to stand till then just hang on" "So who took care of you here?" asked Clove. "Well, mushroom soup will do for supper, and how about some fruits and nuts?" asked Emerald trying to dodge her questions. Clove nodded her head in agreement. "Since I was royal blood, King Oberon and Queen Titania took great care of me, they saw to it that I was raised by the kind Leprechauns. I occasionally go to meet them or whenever they call. You know leprechauns can be mean, or tricksters but thank your stars for finding me." While saying, he was busy preparing the soup and cutting fruits.

"What happened to your stepfamily, the mundane? Did you ever try to find out more about them or your father?" asked Clove. "Yes! I did, my father was known as Mr. Jack Murphy. His wife lived with depression her entire life but I am told he had a daughter named Miss Bridget Murphy she married Mr. Finn Kelly and…" Before

Emerald could complete Clove interrupted him saying, "She had two daughters' one of them was my aunt Camilla." There was pin-drop silence. Both looked at each other in shock, Emerald was the first to walk his way toward Clove. Emerald laid his hands over Clove's head and said, "I know who you are, Apple told me when he was here. He asked me to take you to our island as either you, Aunt Camila's adopted daughter or Aunt Agatha's family member can free my mother. Instead, I choose to free you as one good deed should deserve another. Kindly, be kind to our folk the next time you encounter them. Let the love not be lost. I cannot undo what my mother did but I can hope for forgiveness through you."

The fourth hour had passed and with every passing hour as she took the medicine, her leg improved she could now stand on her feet but was not able to walk. Emerald helped her sit on the toadstool, he put Calendula flower paste on her bruises which slowly began to heal. They had the soup and fruits and the bitterness of the past was put behind them. Emerald told her stories about his numerous encounters with the humans and how he had tricked them. Once a farmer had almost caught him. The farmer had pressured him to reveal the pot of gold to him. He magically gave him a pot of gold which later turned into ashes when he was set free. The hours went by and each hour she got stronger and better. She did not sleep but rather preferred to spend time with him. They spoke about the island, the giants, fairies, and all kinds of magical creatures, and before they knew it was dawn.

"Nice, you guys are having a ball without me," said Apple. Emerald responded, "Well! When the company is good then time flies, have not I told you to knock before you apparated here?" Apple was feasting on the remaining fruits before him, responding "I hate rules." On hearing this they all laughed out loud.

Emerald turned towards Clove and said, "It's time to drop you off, or else it will be difficult to do so when humans are awake. But before that, I want you to look your very best. Just like Cinderella. remodel!" Clove was transformed, she had her hair tied in a ponytail. Her face glowed, and the dress was transformed into a red-and-green combination pinafore dress with black shoes and white socks. "There now you can go." Said Emerald he continued, "Apple will drop you off." "You won't be coming?" "He can't for security reasons," said Apple. "Why worry when I am here? Okay, I hate goodbyes, hold on to my hand it may feel a little nauseous, have a chocolate, that will do you good, here keep this when we get there, eat it." Clove turned her head towards Emerald, to look at him one last time and said, "I wish we could keep meeting." She placed her hand on Apple's and in split seconds before they apparated, she threw her gold ring towards Emerald.

Apple and she were at her grandparents' garden, they had safely apparated but Clove was vomiting. It was her first apparition and it took time for her to adjust. Her head was spinning, she felt light-headed. She went towards the tap and cleaned herself. Apple and she sat down on the grass eating chocolates so that they could not be seen by anyone. Apple spoke up, "Feeling good?" Clove nodded as Apple continued, "Did Emerald tell you about his past?" "Yes, he told me," "Did he tell you about Aunt Camila?" "What about her?" asked Clove. "Oh! Me and my big mouth," said Apple. "Tell me Apple, what are you hiding?" Saying so, she reached out and caught hold of him very tight. The hand which she gripped had the wrought iron ring and his hand began to burn. "Very well! I killed her. Queen Titania instructed me to. We made her write a suicide note so nobody would be suspicious. Your mother met Queen Titania disguised as her. Emerald was not aware of it. When he learned he was upset with

Queen Mother. The sacrifice did not work because she was ill. We needed someone without illness. When Queen Mother learned of you accidentally falling in Emerald's house, you were our next hope. But this time we didn't want to anger Emerald again." "Are there any more secrets?" Asked Clove to which Apple replied, "No, I am sorry." "Then you may leave Apple, I forgive you. But do not erase my memory. I want to keep Emerald's memory with me always and take this secret to the grave with me. Let this be our secret. Let there be no more bloodshed." Clove closed her eyes. She had aged in twenty-four hours. Apple apparated without erasing her memory. Clove got up and walked towards the entrance and she rang the doorbell.

"Emerald, she is safe. I messed up big time. Queen Mother will hang me. Why are you not responding?" anxiously asked Apple. Emerald was seated on the bed and was lost in his thoughts. Clove's ring had bound Emerald to be her slave. There was something about Clove that Emerald felt great, her personality had impressed upon him and now he was beginning to miss her, he wanted to meet her and just see her smile.

Oh! She had made him so comfortable like none before. Apple kept on muttering about his fears but it fell on deaf ears as only Clove was on his mind.

Chapter 17

Home at Last

The butler opened the door. For a second, his expression was as if he had seen a ghost. It took him a fraction of a second to come back to reality. "Is it you Miss Clove or am I dreaming?" asked Donald. Clove had a smile on her face, "Please ring the bell, Yes! It's me!" replied Clove. The butler rang the emergency bell and all the servants of the house, her grandparents, Uncle Connor, Brother James, and her mother came out from their respective rooms.

The mansion echoed with tears of joy. There was jubilation, Clove was back unharmed. Mr. Raven called off the search party informing the concerned authorities. Mrs. Rebecca was busy getting snacks, arranging the bath, and informing all the near and dear ones.

Brother James was thanking the Lord for her safe return. Chloe and Connor hugged her taking her upstairs. They both closed the door and made Clove sit on the bed. Chloe was the first to speak, "Young girl, you owe me an explanation but not today. I want you to freshen up and rest. I will call the physician later in the day to check on you. What matters is you are safe and home with me."

"Mother, I lost my gold ring. I am sorry." Chloe responded, "Listen very carefully, it is you that I am concerned about, there can be many more gold rings. What matters the most is that you are safe. You, my dear, are priceless much worthier than the ring."

Clove was emotional as well as thankful, she had a bath, and ate the snacks her grandmother sent; she was so drained emotionally, physically, and mentally that she fell off to sleep right away in the bed.

"Clove, wake up it is four pm, get ready the physician is here." The governess had resumed her duties and was sent by Chloe to wake her up. Clove was refreshed after the sleep, it did her good. She came downstairs and the physician examined her he could detect only a fracture in the right leg which was healing and advised a plaster. So, he put on a plaster and prescribed minerals & vitamins, taking his leave.

"Clove, we want to know what happened, can you explain yourself?" Chloe asked her daughter. All the members of the family had gathered around her to listen to her side of the story. "Yes, my explanation is long due, I am sorry. I behaved very irresponsibly. When I woke up early in the morning, I decided to go for a bike ride. When I reached the filling station, I saw Grandpa sitting in Uncle Philip's car I followed them. I wanted to get their attention. But in the bargain, I was hit by another vehicle, the next thing I remember is that I tumbled down the cliff and landed in the river. I must have broken my leg then. I lay down on the banks of the river unconscious until a camping family found me. They took care of me and they dropped me nearby. Then I made my way walking to the front door. The rest is history" Clove concluded.

"My child we were there to acquire the neighboring villages and Mr. Philip had something to attend to personally, so we could not stop over. Do you know their names, the family that helped you? They need to be rewarded handsomely." "I am sorry. Grandpa, it slipped my mind, though they did tell me, their son's name was

Emerald and the only word he could say was an apple," "If you do remember something, let me know."

Thereafter Mr. Raven left to go to his study. Uncle Connor carried Clove upstairs to her room, while all went about doing their chores.

Uncle Connor closed the door and said, "Okay! Now can you please tell me what happened?" "You know me very well then why are you asking? Trust me I will tell you when the time is right. Besides, you know I do not hide important matters from you." Clove replied rather mischievously. Connor hugged her, "We were afraid we lost you. Everyone, especially Mom and myself, here were devastated. But now you are here. I have some news for you. Or shall I put it this way? Do you mind me marrying your mother? Would you officially be my daughter?" "Oh! My God! Mom said yes. Aww! Poor Uncle Philip. The grapes are sour for him. When is it?" Clove happily asked Connor warmly hugging him. Connor replied with a smile, "We have planned it next month. It will be a small affair with close-knit family and friends. It will be a civil marriage followed by a Thanksgiving mass and reception at Uncle Philip's renovated hotel." They were distracted by the knock on the door, it was Chloe and she entered the room and sat on the bed. "So, Clove, what's the real story?"

"You didn't buy the story either. "Connor asked, laughing. Clove said, "Please you two, trust me. Let the bygones be bygones. I am here unharmed. That's more important. Let us work together towards a happy future." Chloe interrupted her saying, "Cut the crap. Do not lecture me that is my department. Let us know when you are okay. You have your exams coming up. No matter what happened this year. I want good grades. Never take rash decisions ever again."

There was laughter, fun, and frolic. The entire room was echoing. There was excitement in the air. There was going to be a wedding and with it came lots of shopping. Mrs. Rebecca walked in when they were teasing Connor. She had tears in her eyes, she was so emotional that she thanked God, that Clove was back. The happiness had returned. She asked them to come down for a family supper. She had arranged a picnic for the family at the beach house which meant they had to be in bed early. Clove excused herself and promised to join them later, closing the door of the room after they left.

"Nice story, but it had many loopholes." Clove's eyes widened and turned around to see Emerald sitting on the bed. In her rage, she threw a pillow at him. "Are there more secrets to be revealed?" But Emerald had turned the pillow into rose petals and they fell upon Clove's head. "Nice, so this is how you treat me with anger and I shower you with flowers." Said Emerald. He continued "Didn't you tell them about another wedding." "Who's?" surprisingly asked Clove. "Why did you throw me your fancy finger ring? I am now bound to you till you give me a piece of cloth." "Good, we can keep meeting then, you are the relative I never had." "I love my freedom." Said Emerald. "You are not getting. Till I meet your Queen Titania. She needs to be taught a lesson." "You will always take her name with respect. I will not tolerate disrespect, I am here on a royal errand. Queen Titania has requested an audience with you. She said she needed to speak to you. I will come at midnight as the mundane will be fast asleep. Be ready," said Emerald. "I am not going anywhere." She was angry. "Perhaps I'll turn you into a wristwatch this time. I guess you will be lighter to apparate. The ring stays with me till then. I will give it to you when we switch." Saying this Emerald apparated.

On second thought, Clove wanted to meet this wicked Queen. She had to hear her side of the story. But before that, she had to go down the steps; attend the family dinner, and be normal. Now all she could do was wait for midnight and go with Emerald. She was looking forward to this encounter, God knows what could come out from the Pandora's box this time.

Clove joined the family for dinner. It had been a while since the entire family had joined for dinner. Brother James prayed over and all followed reciting the prayer before the meal. There was laughter along with great food. Everyone was excited about the picnic the next day. But Clove was quietly thinking and contemplating her moves having her dinner, she had lost her appetite and was anxious regarding the meeting. The family discussed the wedding and finalized the guest list.

Mrs. Rebecca asked Clove looking concerned, "What is it? You don't seem interested. Is the food not to your liking or are we a noisy bunch?" Clove replied feeling guilty, "I am not hungry, I just want to rest. If it is okay with all of you." "If it is so then you may take your leave. I will send you a glass of warm milk a little later." Mrs. Rebecca smiled while she said so. Clove thanked everyone, excused herself, and left them and headed towards her room. As she closed the door, she could hear their faint voices. Clove dressed and went to bed, as she lay there waiting for the clock to strike twelve but Alas! she fell asleep.

Chapter 18

Midnight Truths

It was midnight when the cuckoo bird came out to sing the time of the hour, on the other hand, Clove was dead to the world. She was so tired; a lot had happened and many secrets still had to unfold. After the cuckoo bird recoiled back into the clock Emerald appeared. He just snapped his fingers, and a pail of cold water poured water over Clove. "How dare you?" Clove woke up stunned. "Are you out of your mind?" "Oh, did you expect me to shower roses again? Now get up and let us get going we do not have all night." Emerald was irked seeing Clove asleep.

Clove went to the bathroom and got dressed. She came out and was ready to leave. Emerald handed her a chocolate and said, "Here, keep this you may need it. Another thing, in the fairy world you must not eat or drink anything, or else you will lose your memory of your loved ones and will continue to stay there. I have a bag of fruits and water. You will only eat what I give you, so ask me if you are hungry or when you need something just rub the ring you wear on your finger given to you by Aunt Camila and think of what you want in your mind. I will appear to help you. Place your hand on mine we need to apparate soon or we will lose our audience with the king and the queen."

"Oh really! I am dying to meet the murderous queen." Saying so Clove placed her hand on his. "Ouch! That hit me hard. Trust me, you shouldn't have said this."

Emerald snapped his fingers and Clove was transfigured into a crow. "I guess this should teach you a lesson to mellow down your temper and never speak ill of anyone." Clove was erratically flying and cawing in the room. It was evident that she detested the change and wanted her original self-back. Emerald had his laugh and when he was done he transformed her back. "Don't you ever do this to me again." Clove was filled with rage. Emerald replied, "It is time to go and I guess we both have learned our lessons well." Clove placed her hand on Emerald's and then they apparated.

Emerald brought Clove to a deserted island. As they touched down Clove was vomiting a little yet again. She was handed a chocolate by him. The apparition made her sick every time. She was getting used to it and did better every time. As she lay down on the beach eating her chocolate and looking at the stars, the cold breeze soothed her; she mustered the courage and asked Emerald, "Where are we? What's to be done next."

Emerald had a spark in his eyes, he looked happy, "You are in the Kingdom of the Sky. This is my home. Let me give you a little tour. We have time before the audience." Saying this he got up and lent a hand to Clove. Clove distrustful ignored him and got up by herself. She then dusted herself and was good to go. Emerald eagerly spoke, "So I will give you the aerial tour of our island." Before she could respond Emerald had caught her hand and they had taken off. The island appeared to be butterfly-shaped from above. The landscapes were rugged, there was a waterfall at the center of the island. There were hills to the north which looked green from above. The island had territories marked with walls. Each territory had a different color sparks symbolizing different magical creatures. Towards the north of the Island, she could see a castle. Emerald yelled out, "That's

King Oberon's castle, we are headed there." He dived with her and they had a soft landing in front of the castle gates. The castle gates were huge with a huge wooden door. It had a pulley and when the ropes were pulled; the door opened. The guards inspected Emerald's wand and sword, they bowed down and said," Forgive us, your Highness! it's our routine check to avoid imposters, we see you have company?" "Yes! I will subject her ring. I have this parchment stating her audience with the Queen." Saying this he took out a rather old-looking yellow parchment and asked Clove to show her the ring that was given to her by Camilla. When they touched it with their wands glowed, they bowed before Clove. "Your Highness! You may pass." The guards moved aside. Emerald and Clove walked past them. The place was crowded with fair folk. The fairies wore pretty gowns, their hair in buns, all the men were handsome and radiant in their suits. Emerald was well known among them as it was obvious everyone curtsied to him and made way for him. As they were entering the palace, Apple bumped into Emerald. "There you are! Right on the dot. The Queen has asked an audience in her room. This must be important very few get entrance and to allow this mundane it would be big for all of us. Follow me sire." He led the way to the Queen's chamber.

"Whatever your differences, Clove, you must be courteous and must curtsey to Queen Mother. Or arrogance can take you down." Emerald was whispering into Clove's ears admonishing her. After seeing his welcome Clove did not want to mess it up. Her wait was over, she had reached the chambers and they were waiting for Apple to let them in. When the time was right Apple approached them and they were permitted. "You will bow your head and not look her in the eyes unless you are spoken to. You will reply and then continue to bow your head." Apple was looking for a head nod from

Clove. Clove winked her eyes, bowed her head, and entered the room along with Emerald.

"Emerald! There you are I have been eagerly waiting for you," said Queen Mother as she extended her right hand. Emerald after curtseying went forward and kissed her on the hand. "Your Majesty, the pleasure is mutual, I have brought in your presence Ms. Clove as you expressed a desire to have your audience with her." "Yes, I very well see she has come, Emerald." Saying this the Queen arose from her chair and asked for privacy. When the servants left Queen Mother said, "You can be at ease Clove, it is just us." Clove raised her head and paid the Queen Mother her curtsy. She then raised her head to look in her eyes. The Queen Mother was fair as snow, she had the radiance or a halo surrounding her, she wore a coppery shimmering dress, her hair was in a bun, and she had a motherly aura around her. Clove was confused about how a motherly figure like her could kill her aunt, there was surely some mistake.

The Queen Mother spoke, "Clove, I hope it is okay for you if I address you this way." Clove silently nodded. The Queen Mother continued to speak, "I must say life has been hard on you and you have lost your loved ones, but I see and hear from Emerald that you are an embodiment of strength and courage. There are some truths, I want you to know. Come let us sit and talk through this." She walked through the room towards the couch where they could sit across and talk. Emerald and Clove followed her through and took their places across each other. The Queen Mother spoke, "Clove, I am not sure of how much you know but let's start from the beginning so things are clear between us. I don't know how much you and Emerald are aware but I know you know things in bits and pieces. My sister Princess Mab was taking a stroll at the beach when she found your great grandfather, Mr.

Jack Murphy whose boat had crashed on our island's shore, he was lying unconscious but alive. Princess Mab fell in love with a mundane, Mr. Jack Murphy your supposed great grandfather. It was indeed love at first sight; pure and selfless love. She stood at his side and nursed him until he recovered. He was too weak and needed nourishment, he was fed our food. As a result, he lost his memory for a brief period and in that period, he reciprocated towards her advances. They courted for months and chose to take this relationship to the next level. They approached us for their blessings to be wed but, we refused as we didn't want a mundane in our midst. We were not sure of his life before he turned up. My sister Mab was hurt, sad, and pained by the decision we took. My husband sent word to the neighboring kingdoms for suitors. One, in particular, pleased the King, he was Prince Angus. He seemed perfect as he had eternal youth and charm. He ruled well, the perfect suitor. When my sister Princess Mab was introduced to him he accepted the marriage proposal. But since my sister had lost her heart to Mr. Jack Murphy, she did not take to well his advances which offended him. Prince Angus was offended and outraged, he could not bear that he was rejected despite his looks, royalty, and riches. He went back to the mainland and tried to collect information about your great-grandfather from the locals and one day on purpose he bumped into Mrs. Honora Murphy, Jack's wife. Mrs. Honora Murphy was oblivious to his malicious intentions. He slowly befriended her and found out that they were happily married and she along with her daughter Bridget who was 2 years old awaited his return from the sea as he was a fishmonger. Prince Angus then did the most horrendous act. He kidnapped and brought their daughter Bridget to the fairy world. It was when Mr. Jack saw Bridget that reminiscence of his past life flashed back. By then it was too late as Princess Mab and Mr. Jack

Murphy were married and she was with a child who you know now as Emerald." Queen Mother stopped to drink water. Clove and Emerald were distressed at the discovery.

Emerald never knew the truth, everything was passed down through word of mouth and thus the story got distorted. He was happy that he could know the actual truth as he was always shy about asking the truth to Queen Mother and when approached she always told him when the time was right she would let him know. Clove was trying to sink in this information as she felt it was too much for her. Queen Mother cleared her throat. "Sorry about that my throat got a little dry, so, where was I? Yes, Mr. Jack Murphy begged him not to harm her. Since my sister married a mundane she was given a mediocre home at the far end of the island and was stripped of all titles living like a mundane without any help. This was a much-regretted decision, I think we made which changed the course of numerous lives. Prince Angus took advantage of this as he knew they had no help. He returned Bridget to Jack on one condition that he had to leave Princess Mab for good. Jack was blinded by the love of his child and agreed to his demands. But Prince Angus betrayed him. He took Jack with his daughter to the mainland and killed him in front of his wife. His wife couldn't take this too well and she lived in depression. While Bridget was taken care of by us. We kept a nanny from the fairy world who took care of her. Bridget had magical powers but chose not to exercise them. Once, she came of age and married the protection was lifted but we gave her a magical ring to be worn which rests on your finger so that she could summon the fairyland whenever she wanted to return. But she never did, however, she saw a magical spark in your aunty Camilla and she passed on the ring to her without actually letting her know the true worth and purpose of it. I guess she wanted to take this information to her grave as she had lived the worst consequences. Camilla unknowingly did well at cooking as that was the only skill her mother passed down to her. She was good."

Clove interrupted, "Forgive me, Your Highness, why did you kill her?" Queen Mother appeared to be shocked "Oh! Good Lord, do you think that I could do it? Apple tricked you so that would be enough motivation for you to meet me. It had nothing to do with me. It was King Angus." Clove widened her eyes she was in shock as Queen Mother spoke, "My sister lies hidden in his kingdom because he forcefully abducted her, after killing Jack and leaving Emerald to us to care for. Emerald is not a Leprechaun but a cursed fairy by King Angus and he can transform when his mother is freed as the curse would break by performing a rite. Whenever we sent our fairies, they would be caught or intercepted thus we need to break through with an Eerie." Emerald interrupted Queen Mother, "Pardon me, Aunt, why did King Angus kill her aunt and what is an Eerie?" Queen Mother replied, "Emerald, the ring offers protection, when Camilla gave the ring to Clove, the protection went to Clove leaving her exposed, he will not leave any surviving member from that family with a magical power as they are a threat to him and he can die. Emerald, in our Fairy world we call an Eerie the one who has one mundane parent and the other one from the magical folk. Clove there is something, I am not the right person to tell you but the time has come when you should know this. Camilla was your biological mother, she conceived you out of wedlock and so your foster parents adopted you. But till today it is a mystery as to who your father was. Two people knew the truth. One was Camila and the other was Charles and they have both left the world.

When she gave you to them, she made a promise that they would not have their own. Connor got married to her as a good friend and took responsibility despite loving Chloe. Camilla could never conceive again as both Connor and she had health issues preventing conception." "So not true, I do not believe you." Queen Mother continued, "Clove, I have something that will prove to you that what I am saying is true, let's walk over to the magical seeing bowl." Saying this Queen Mother arose with them as they walked towards the magical seeing bowl. The bowl was shaped like human hands carved out of marble joining together to hold a clear liquid. Queen Mother raised her wand and a vial containing hair appeared towards her from nowhere. Looking at Clove, Queen Mother asked," Do you recognize this hair?" Clove took a closer look at it and exclaimed it to be Aunt Camilla's hair. Queen Mother asked Clove to put her ring in the bowl and then she put one strand of hair. Queen Mother said, "This will show you the important events of Camila's life." After a few seconds, her entire life and memories flashed before her eyes, only if she knew that Camilla was her mother she would hug her one last time and affectionately call her mom. Clove, broke down crying. She could not believe that the aunt she loved so dearly was indeed her mother.

Queen Mother Consoled Clove "Sometimes the truth can be painful but the sooner we accept it, the better it gets to deal with it. Collect yourself together. You were hers and thus she gave you the ring. Won't you avenge her death? You can break the curse and free my sister. We need you the most, you should be at your best." Emerald breaks his silence, "I perfectly understand that you are scared, and hurt and have lately gone through a lot. I am okay with you not wanting to fight our battle. But never forget you are not alone in this. I can understand the pain that you are going through. Because I thought my mother never existed and now she is in captivity for so many years."

Queen's Mother interrupted with a sorrowful voice, "Clove, you will not be alone, Apple and Emerald will be with you, you will be given the dagger of your grandfather which he received from the King on his marriage, Princess Mab's wand and all sorts of magical items to help you. You can teleport to safety anytime you feel you are in danger with the gifted enchanted ring left by your mother. You will never be alone at all costs. I want you to know, I arrived late that fateful night. By the time I could reach her, she was dead am sorry, I wish I had known sooner."

Clenching the vial, with determination and vengeance Clove finally said. "Fine, I am ready."

Chapter 19

Deliverance

"Why me, always? Why do I have to be the scapegoat?" saying this Apple was dodging all the magical spells that Clove learned to self-guard herself. Emerald wanted her to practice and learn the basic magical spells which she would need, he also gave her a miniature version of the book. She learned to use teleportation through the use of the ring and the dagger. They were practicing at Princess Mab's house. In fairyland, Emerald always stayed there. He would go to her bedroom, touch her clothes, and smell them to know what she smelt like, that was all he had of her.

"Very good! Clove you have outdone yourself," exclaimed Emerald. "That means I am free." Said Apple. All three chuckled. They were bonding during the practice sessions and Apple always made them laugh.

"Your Highness, pardon me, Queen Mother has requested an audience this very instance. She has got very urgent news to share." Said a maid. "I do not like the sound of it," said Apple. "Nonsense! We'll be there soon," said Emerald. On hearing this, the maid left. The three gathered what they needed and Clove teleported them to the entrance of the door to her chambers with the help of the ring. By now, Clove had practiced and Emerald was proud of her.

"You may go inside, she is ready to receive you." The maid ushered them inside, she walked out and closed the door behind her. All three curtsied and Emerald approached her, "Oh! I have great news. Queen Mother, Clove has outdone herself. She has perfected every spell and is ready for the ordeal." Emerald exclaimed.

Queen Mother replied, "That is indeed great news. I brought you here to tell you two things, firstly no one suspects that Clove has been here with us for the past fifteen days because I have placed a fairy there so they do not get worried about Clove's absence, all are doing just fine, the wedding shopping has begun and your grades are improving in school. Secondly, I befriended Queen Diana, she is the wife of King Angus. Now you have to know what you are dealing with before we attack. She hates him, he has been evil to his subjects, she cannot tolerate him any further, and wants Princess Mab freed as she is jealous of her. Princess Mab is well and very well taken care of by King Angus, he visits her chambers twice, she is held captive in a glass room, and enchanted salt is sprayed around the glass so no fairy can approach except him. Her chamber lies to the north of his castle. He feels victorious every time he visits her like she is his trophy. Today, at midnight is when you three will break in because King Angus is out visiting the water kingdom ruled by King Alford. Queen Diana, will help you break in. You will free Princess Mab and come back safely then we will think of a way to deal with King Angus."

"You are telling me to just run away without killing him?" interrupted Clove. Emerald spoke up reasoning with Clove, "We need better preparation to fight him. We need to free Princess Mab as then we will be in a better position. We will get help from other kingdoms. If we kill him that will not win hearts for now. If we fail in our attempt he could be very mean to her."

Queen Mother spoke calmly, "We will avenge his actions, with precision and preparation. We need to free Princess Mab first. Queen Diana will signal the next move when the time is right. She wants her son on the throne. That is the deal. Earth fairies are associated with humans so they are harsh and have more negative emotions. We have to be very careful with what we do, even our dealings with Queen Diana. Queen Diana has promised to meet you at the North End of the Castle, her maid will bring you in. At midnight the guards change, and she will bring in her fairy for us, who will sneak you in up to the North End of the Castle. Queen Diana, has sent us the Hag Stone Amulet, this is what King Angus uses to meet Princess Mab. He has gone to procure it from King Alford."

Emerald takes it in his hands and looks at it closely, "What is this? I have not seen it before?" Queen Mother informs him by saying, "This is made up of a stone found naturally on the beaches with a hole in the center, it is very rare to find it, this can be placed on salt or salt water and break the power of salt and strengthen the fairy. Princess Mab's powers are weakened with the salt around her, you must place the bracelet on her hand by doing so. You give her back her powers. I shall meet you at dawn with good news. Please make us proud. Another thing, I would want to give you an amethyst ring, the stone looks purple and it's a type of quart which has radioactivity when it touches iron. Clove you will have to rub this on your ring collect everyone and teleport. The effect will last a minute so the radiation will blind all the Earth fairies exclusively."

Queen Diana had confirmed his exit and the trios were now ready to apparate and complete their mission. Queen Mother had wished them luck, she hugged Emerald as she was fond of him as she had none of her own. They had reached the hideout eagerly waiting for the signal.

"I guess this is it, let us watch over them from the distance and when the time is right we will go," said Apple. All three were distantly watching the guards and waiting for them to change. It was around midnight. "There, the guards are changing. But where is our help?" curious Clove enquired. "Patience is the key," said Emerald. King Angus's castle was placed in an Oak tree. From the outside, it looked like a huge bark but inside the hole, it was all enchanted and huge. After a while a fairy appeared, her eyes lit all green, and green light emitted from her eyes, lighting the path for them. "That is the signal let us go folks. On second thought, she is dating material. How will we look together?" Apple inquired. "Yeah, if we escape alive. You might just want to be grateful." Said Emerald. "God, who would want to date that girl with scary eyes?" asked Clove. "Unfortunately, that would be me." Apple mocked his taste.

They approached the entrance and they were greeted by the guards and the fairy. Apple was pleased to give his introduction but he was not able to make a lasting impression on the fairy, she seemed emotionless and least interested. They were checked and were asked to keep Clove's dagger, also Emerald, and Apple's swords behind. They swore they would not use it first, only for self-defense. So, the dagger and swords were enchanted so that they would not be used first and they followed the fairy inside. As they were inside the castle what looked like a small hole never seemed to end. There was a garden surrounding the castle which lay within, the fairy took them towards the North. The entrance had tall trees with guards on top of them, they were followed from the top till they reached the doorway. "You will enter the door and take the wooden stairs which spiral to the top.

Everything is enchanted so please do not touch anything. Queen Diana awaits you at the door to the chambers of Princess Mab. Make haste." Said the fairy. "Why are you not coming?" asked Apple. "I am following my orders to escort you to the door." "Now please hurry." Saying this she left discretely. "Could it be a trap?" Questioned Apple. "Time will tell, let me go first then followed by Clove and you follow her," Said Emerald.

They took the stairs as they were told by the maid and found different enchantments like portraits, gems, fruits, metals, swords, and infant fire-breathing dragons. But they quietly climbed the stairs without touching or interacting with them, they stopped when they saw Queen Diana at the top. All curtsied to her. "Greetings your Highness, we come in peace and love," Said Emerald. "Greetings Prince Emerald, I hope you have not touched anything on your way as they are all teleporting keys to different parts of the castle and if used or touched, they will alert King Angus," asked Queen Diana visibly anxious. "Yes, your majesty, we haven't touched anything." Replied Emerald. "Very well, let us finish the deal." Queen Diana was nervous. They followed her to the door which she magically opened with her voice command, it was a big airy room, there were pink and white curtains hanging on the windows. In the middle of the room, Princess Mab was enclosed in a glass enclosure. She had her bed, table chair, and a brick wall which would be the closet and bathing area. She looked teary-eyed and sad. She was lost in deep thoughts oblivious to their presence. Only they could see her, she could not even hear them. She heard only King Angus's voice. He often would speak to her across the glass.

Emerald was teary-eyed but his happiness knew no bounds. He wanted to hug his mother. Queen Diana broke Emerald's chain of thoughts saying, "Use the amulet and enter and quickly make haste before the king comes." Clove wore the hag stone amulet and crossed the ring of the salt, she touched the glass door, and when the door opened she quickly went to Princess Mab. "Your Highness, please make haste we need to go to the Island of Sky, your son has come to take you with him," said Clove. Princess Mab arose and caught her hand. "Who are you?" Clove told her to trust and gave her the amulet as they were exiting through the glass door, they heard a loud voice sounding angry, "I smell two, I can let only one or give me blood." Now when a fairy loses blood their powers weaken and they can be easily attacked. King Angus was smart enough to use dark magic. Princess Mab told Clove to head with the amulet first and she would give her blood as she is smarter, older, and has more experience. Clove handed her wand to her and her husband's dagger. Clove crossed the salt ring, returning safely and the door closed behind her. Once the Princess saw that she had crossed over, she took her husband's dagger, wounded her left forearm and as the blood trickled down the hand on the floor she muttered a spell, and the door opened. "You can go now," said the voice which had calmed after receiving the blood offering. The door opened and as she was crossing the salt ring the drops of blood from her wounded hand fell on it, the room lit up with radiant green light, and all were blinded within seconds King Angus and his guards appeared, and the blood that touched the salt ring was enchanted to signal a break in. Each of them was tagged with one guard and their hands were tied behind their backs with creepers and wands on the side of the neck ready to curse them. King Angus spoke with a mischievous tone, "Well! Let's see who we have a cursed prince, a leprechaun, and Jack's granddaughter. To what I owe your presence, Princess Mab, do you think I would let you go that easily? My darling wife, you dare to free her. Time has come to nip your wings; I shall deal with you later, once I get rid of the uninvited guests. Guards, I declare her a traitor and put her in the dungeons." The guard immediately escorted Queen Diana outside the room.

Princess Mab pleaded, "Angus, it is I that you want to let them leave in peace. I will stay back as long as you want." Saying this she had tears in her eyes. Prince Angus responded, "Where is that arrogance Mab? All these years you despised me, all I wanted was kind words and affection. But you spat on me, cursed me, and enraged me, you never reciprocated my love. Now are you softening because of these children?"

Clove interrupted him saying, "Love, how can you say that? You are such a coward, a murderer, so self-obsessed, how can you know the true meaning of love." King Angus smiled, "You mundane, I like your confidence, do not think that I cannot kill you, it will not take me a minute. But I do not count on you. It is Emerald I am interested in. It will be great fun to torture a son in front of his mother." Princess Mab pleaded sighing, "Angus, please let the children go."

While all the commotion was going on Apple untied himself, freeing himself from the guard. Seeing the commotion Clove's guard rushed over leaving her unattended, she rubbed the rings and the room was clouded in purple dust in split seconds Emerald, Princess Mab, and Apple all ran towards Clove, while she apparated along with others King Angus with his wand threw a spell towards Emerald, Apple seeing his move came in between and was hit with the spell. It was too late they had gone but Apple was hurt. All had teleported. They vaguely heard King Angus's frustrating yell behind them. They knew he would not rest. But for now, they were safe.

Clove brought them to Queen Mother's chambers as per her instructions, Apple was bleeding profusely, he had lost a lot of blood. So was Princess Mab, both were shifted to the hospital wing. Apple could not withstand the curse, his soul perished leaving jasmine flowers behind. On the magical island of the Sky, the magical folk left their world with their favorite flowers behind. Princess Mab was recovering with the portions that were given to her.

Emerald was sad tonight; he lost his friend, though they were an unlikely pair, they had a very special bond. Clove comforted him, in silence in a way that she could understand his pain. They both were seated on the beach holding hands looking at the sky; Emerald was grieving his friend's loss while Clove was offering him his condolences in silence. Clove was the first to break the silence. "I am truly heartbroken about the loss of your friend. Words feel so inadequate at a time like this, but please know that I am here for you in every possible way. Your strength and resilience have always amazed me, and I know you will find the courage to navigate through this difficult time. Lean on me whenever you need to, cry if you must, and remember that your friend's spirit will always live on in the beautiful memories you shared." Emerald, broke down sobbing saying, "Honestly I knew there was danger, it feels like a part missing, it hurts even more to know he died saving me. This will be a burden upon me. Thank you, I feel lost, it's just I feel he will spring out of nowhere to irritate me and a part of me tells me he is no more."

Emerald laid his head on Clove's lap while Clove gently stroked his hair, offering silent comfort in the warmth of her touch. As she continued to stroke his hair, her touch conveyed a sense of safety and solace. With each gentle caress, she silently reassured him of her unwavering presence and support offering him a beacon of hope amidst the darkness, guiding him through the depths of his grief with her boundless love.

Two days later, Princess Mab recovered and King Oberon, Queen Mother with the help of Princess Mab broke the spell over Emerald through a rite and he turned into a handsome fairy. He was declared to be the crown prince by King Oberon and to mark this day a three-day feast was held in the Kingdom. All the fairies took part in it. Royal Guests from other kingdoms came to preside over the festivities. All the kingdoms big and small made a truce and promised to execute King Angus in the event of him harming any fairy folk of the Kingdom of Sky. They extended their protection to Clove a mundane as she had shown great courage in helping the fairy folk.

Emerald and Clove danced all night. Princess Mab had dressed her in one of her evening gowns and Emerald could not take his eyes off her.

But their happiness had to end. She had to go back and return to her kind. While he had to perform his duties. Although the fear of King Angus lurked in the background. He was imprisoned and his son took over the throne. Queen Diana was unfortunately executed by him. The fairy world was rejoicing as goodness prevailed.

"This is it. We are back to square one," said Emerald to Clove. "I hate to say this, but I surely will miss you." Saying this Emerald hugged Clove. Clove was silent and teary-eyed. Deep down she knew that this day would come, she had to return home. As they were in her bedroom, she hoped that time would stand still forever. "I will miss you too. I wish we could be together." In between her sobs, Clove finally said what was in her heart. Emerald seated her on the bed and said, "Clove,

King Angus, he is in captivity and I do not know for how long. He is vicious and I need to keep you away from the limelight. You will be safe here and go unnoticed, I do not know my foes and friends only time will tell. I will come to meet you when you call for me. But you will never visit the Kingdom of Skye until I am sure you will be safe. I have things to deal with my folk, I want to spend some time with my mother. I have to strengthen ties with other kingdoms" "OK! Now stop lecturing. How about I turn you into a nightingale, at least this would be musical." Clove was smiling and Emerald followed her with a smile. "Indeed, any fowl is better than a crow." They both laughed. "Do you still think King Angus could harm me or your folk anyway?" anxiously asked Clove. "As long as King Angus lives, there is a chance." Saying this Emerald paused, he held her hand again, and meeting each other's gaze with conviction he continued, "You changed my life, I found my mother, I am indebted to you, and I will guard you with my life. But King Angus attacking can be a possibility, slim yes, but should never be taken lightly."

Chapter 20

Wedding Bells

After days of planning and precision, today Connor was to wed Chloe in a civil wedding. They decided to go for a 10 am Civil Wedding with the Thanksgiving mass at 11 am in church and have a Reception later at Banquet Hall, at Black Orchid Hotel which belonged to Philip and was redecorated by Chole. Both wanted a close-knit low-key celebration. Although there was a difference in opinion the couple had won the battle and the rest wanted them to enjoy their big day. Clove was happy for them and she did miss Emerald and wished he could be a part of this celebration but he was a hidden secret she did not want to disclose yet as she felt that the time had not come yet. Chloe let her hair down with a red roses wreath on her head as she ditched the veil and her dress was made of ivory-colored silk material with three-quarter-length sleeves with an open boat neckline. The dress was without lace or any other embellishments. Chloe held a round bouquet with twenty roses and no foliage. Connor wore a blue colored suit with a blue tie and an ivory-color shirt. The guests from the bride's side wore maroon and the guests from the bridegroom's side wore blue. Clove wore a bottle-green cocktail dress. The couple looked the best. The photographer was hired and he was busy taking the pictures until the couple was called by the officiant.

The officiant welcomed everyone and introduced the ceremony. He gave a brief explanation of the purpose and significance of marriage. The officiant asked Connor "Do you, Conner Burns take Chloe Campbell to be your lawful wedded wife?" To which he replied, "I Do."

The officiant asked Chloe, "Do you, Chloe Campbell take Conner Burns to be your lawful wedded husband?" He then continued to ask the couple one at a time, "Do you, promise to love, honor, and cherish the other for as long as you both shall live?" to which the couple replied affirmatively.

He asked them to take their vows to which Chloe proclaimed, "I, Chloe Campbell, take you, Connor Burns to be my wedded husband to have and to hold from this day forward, for better or for worse, for richer or for poorer, in sickness and in health, to love and to cherish, until death do us part." Connor wrote his vows and he said looking into Chloe's eyes, "Before I met you, I felt like nobody understood me, but then you came along, it was like you already knew my language, I got addicted to you so easily, attracted to you in ways that are hard to explain. It immediately felt important like this was someone I needed in my life, today I think I need to express how deeply grateful I am for you, I have no idea what I would have done this far without you. We have shared so many great moments, laughing until our stomachs hurt, smiling just because we are together, staying up all night, and having our 3 am snack, I have always heard people finding that once-in-a-lifetime kind of love. They say how your soulmate will also be your best friend, to tell you the truth I have not related to something so much, I am pretty sure I have found it and now I wish to cherish this till death do us part.

The officiant on hearing the Connor's vows was moved with emotion and so were all in the room, he asked the couple to exchange rings, symbolizing their commitment and they said, "With this ring, I thee wed, and with it, I bestow upon thee all the treasures of my mind, heart, and hands."

With a smile on his face he continued to say, "By the authority vested in me by the State, I now pronounce you husband and wife. You may kiss each other."

Connor seized the opportunity to kiss his bride. While all the guests cheered for them, the couple, along with the officiant and witnesses, signed the marriage register.

He congratulated the couple by wishing them, "May your marriage be filled with love, laughter, and happiness. Congratulations to the newlyweds! It is my great honor and privilege to present to you, for the first time, Mr. and Mrs. Connor and Chloe Burns. The photographer captured all the moments but what he could not was the feeling of total bliss that finally two souls found their way back together.

The mass thereafter was solemn and then they had a grand party at the renovated hotel for the 200 guests that the couple approved. Chloe's entire family was there. Connor's brother was there at his side. Camila's sister came to wish them luck. Arthur had made it to wish them both. Philip with his dad was present. Fr. Tony, Aunt Pamela, Patrick, Ryan, and their neighbor's family and friends. The guests liked the ambience and Chloe's much effort on the renovation front was much appreciated.

"Congratulation! Madam." Arthur wished Chloe. "Thank you!" replied Chloe. "If you don't mind may I tell you something." "What is it Arthur?" inquired Chloe. "Madam, I vaguely remember, Charles, had once confided in me that your father wanted to bring you back home and poison your mind against him, get you divorced, and marry you to Mr. Philip. This was disclosed to Sir, just in time before Connor sold everything. That is why Charles did not shift because he did not want to lose you. Today I am happy that you ended with Connor rather than Mr. Philip." "Why didn't you let me know this earlier? Rather why now?" "Because I just remembered so looking at Mr. Philip," replied Arthur.

Meanwhile, Philip clicked on his glass of champagne and gave the toast saying " One day you meet someone and for some inexplicable reason, you feel more connected to this stranger than anyone else, even closer to them than your closet family, perhaps this person carries within them an angel, that is sent to you for some higher purpose, it could be to teach you an important lesson or keep you safe through a perilous time, what one must do is to trust in them, even if they bring along pain or suffering, the reason for their presence will become clear in due time, and eventually, you grow to love this person. Cheers! to finding this in each other. I wish you both a happy married life especially my dear friend Chloe." Philip raised his glass and all drank the champagne after he had clinked his glass with the couple.

There were cheers all around and with the music played Conner danced with Chloe. Chole then danced with Mr. Raven. She then slowly whispered in his ears, "Dad, sorry your match turned out to be my friend. Disappointed, aren't you?" "Any man would do but Charles, because he took you away from us. I was angry, clouded but now your happiness is all that matters." Replied Mr. Raven.

Seeing everyone busy, Clove missed Emerald. "Do you miss me that bad?" Clove heard a familiar male voice. When she turned towards it, she saw Emerald serving drinks in a waiter's uniform. She got up and cornered him, "Oh my God! What are you doing here?" "Isn't it rude, I rather thought you would welcome me with open arms?" Emerald, sarcastically said so. "I wasn't missing you, you think very highly of yourself." Snubbed Clove. "Oh! Girls I tell you, they don't know what they want, then I think I should be dancing with Aunty Pamila's granddaughter, your playmate. I have taken a fancy to her." Teasingly Emerald started to move in her direction. "Don't you dare, I am warning you?" Clove held Emerald's arms and pulled him towards her. "Let go of me, they are searching for you." Emerald apparated in time as Rebecca came to call Clove for it was time the bride would toss the bouquet and they were leaving for their honeymoon.

Chloe and Connor got busy with both businesses. Clove went to school and lived her life, Emerald visited her whenever she rubbed her ring. Life continued for all.

Five years had passed, and Clove asked Conner on their way to the grocery store, "Dad did you love my mother?" Conner looked confused and asked, "I did not understand your question. Could you reframe it?" Clove told him that she knew that Camilla was her biological mother, she wanted to know if he loved her or compromised just because Chloe chose Charles.

"How on earth did you discover this? I forgot this. It has been so long." Connor was shocked. "Does it matter who told me, what matters is the question at the moment," Clove replied. Connor although surprised that she knew the truth told her that he was attracted to Chloe initially but Camila taught him what real love was he told her that he never regretted marrying her. He was lucky that he fell in love and was married twice to the people he loved and hoped, she too would find love.

Clove smiled to herself looking at the side mirror of the car, in her heart, she knew she had fallen in love but it was time for Emerald to know, as tonight she was eighteen and her parents had planned a birthday party which was being celebrated later in the day, after which she had to break the news to him as she would be visiting the Island of Sky, after midnight there was a ceremony kept in her honor. She was coming of age and had to choose between magic and her world. Although the ride was quite silent, inside her heart firecrackers were bursting and she was excited to propose to Emerald.

Chapter 21

Change of Plans

Clove had put on an evening gown. It was Camila's as Clove wanted to wear it to her eighteenth birthday bash. The dress was altered to fit her, she looked pretty as she waited for her make-up artist to apply make-up and do her hair. She stopped in front of the mirror to just check herself out. It was a big day, she wanted to soak it all in. If only Camila was here, these five years she missed her so much. They visited her grave every year on Camila's birth and death anniversaries.

"Hmm! You look great," said Emerald. Clove's eyes widened, and she was shocked. "Turn around, I am not done yet. You ruined the surprise," a shocked Clove blurted out. "There isn't all that time. Clove, you need to come with me. King Angus has escaped from the dungeons and along with him two other fairies. We can't let you be unattended. It can be dangerous. The party needs to be canceled. God knows how many mundane can die today. It can turn into a blood bath if you do not listen."

"Just wait here I need to change into something more comfortable. I need to explain to my parents do you understand I am not a kid anymore," replied Clove angrily.

Hearing her reply Emerald snapped his fingers, the gown turned into blue denim jeans and a white shirt. Her hair was neatly tied into a ponytail. Her dagger was in her right pocket, her wand was in her left. Her iron wrought ring was on her finger and she had her sneakers on. Vexed Clove asked Emerald if he would teleport her parents too sarcastically. He declined her offer which irked her more as he did not quite catch her mood. As she smirked, sensing he did something wrong Emerald undid the last spell. "Will you stop that!" Clove yelled at him walking out of the room back in a gown.

Clove walked towards her parent's room and when she approached the door, she knocked on it. "Come in," Connor answered. She opened the door and stood there. Connor was speechless looking at her in Camila's dress. "Dear me, you remind me of her. But you need to do something about your hair and maybe some lipstick." Connor was wearing his tie when he said so. "Where is mom?" asked Clove. "She is taking a quick shower. We will be done in 40 minutes," replied Connor while he was finishing his knot and looking in the mirror.

"Dad, could you do me a favor? Can you cancel this party? I beg you to do so." Clove pleaded. Connor paused walking towards his daughter. "What is the matter? You can trust me sweetheart whatever the matter is please tell me freely. We are here to help you." Saying this Connor was walking towards Clove, laying his hand on her head. Clove was in tears, politely asking him to fetch her mom and come to her room.

After a while, both her parents arrived at her room and were seated on the bed. They were angry, wondering who Emerald was, and what he was doing in their house. Emerald greeted them. First, he introduced himself and told them the whole story in brief. Chole was worried for Clove as King Angus was on the loose, while Connor was amazed at what Clove had been through yet, he was anxious because he did not want to lose her as he sensed danger.

Connor was the first to speak among them, "OK, you are sure if I cancel today's party then it will be safer as the guests won't be harmed. But what about the rest of us?" To which Emerald replied, "With due respect sir, we have a safe hideout for you all. You will be placed with Leprechauns who took care of me. We will teleport you there, nevertheless, your servants have to be split. For I know King Angus if he finds an empty house. He will suspect foul play. Choose your staff well those who will accompany you; they should be loyal to you at all times. The rest need not know your whereabouts." Connor inquired further, "May I ask where will we be teleported?" Emerald replied, "To the Oak Tree in the backyard of Campbell Cottage." Chloe was quick to respond, "What! My house, since how long have they been there?" Emerald replied, "Charles's grandfather once caught a Leprechaun while burying gold in his backyard when the afraid Leprechaun begged for his life, Grandpa in return told him not to worry as he was kind and benevolent. He gave the Leprechaun space to live freely in the Oak tree then only would he let go of him and since then the Leprechaun has never let the Campbell family turn poor. The pact was made to never to cut the tree and all true heirs are told to do so."

Chloe was in shock, as this was news to her. As danger was lurking, she only had her gut feeling, she had to trust Clove and rely on Emerald to save the day. But at the end of it, will everyone make it safe was something that truly scared her.

Chloe instructed the butler Donald and the driver were instructed to take a cook, a housekeeping staff, food supplies, and whatever essentials and personal belongings to the Campbell house by road. Meanwhile, Connor had assembled Chloe, her parents, and her brother, all into Clove's bedroom they had a small family briefing, Grandfather Raven was not happy about the change, and Rebecca was anxious. Father James was confident about Clove. Clove held on to her dagger and asked all to hold on to her tightly. On the count of three, she apparated with them.

They were all standing in the backyard in front of the oak tree. Everyone was nauseous. "My God! You are a pro, my dear," said Chloe. "My good gracious God, how would we get into it? I see no burrow," exclaimed Rebecca. Clove removed the protective enchantments and the burrow appeared. She placed a ladder by the flick of her wand which helped them get into the burrow one at a time. On entering, Clove covered the burrow with her protective spells. As she turned, Emerald was waiting there for them. Connor was speechless. What looked so small was huge inside. The drawing area was well-lit with the sunlight. There were toadstools for sitting and an "L" shaped couch made from a log and bearskin. The dining area had a table with small chairs. Several rooms were opening from the drawing room. The first leprechaun had a big nose serving fruit juice and had a white shirt with Bignose embroidered in red. The second one was having small feet serving the tarts and he had Paddy embroidered in green. As they entered, they were served fruit juice and tarts. Father James had lost his appetite. While Rebecca was gorging her tarts, they tasted so yummy.

Emerald spoke first, "We meet again, I guess you all are doing fine so far. We have Bignose and Paddy here to help you with whatever you will need. Meanwhile, I will take Clove along with me to the Island of Sky. All the kingdoms will unite against King Angus, he will not stand a chance. But please be together and no matter what, do not leave this place at any cost. I will give you a safe word whenever you see Clove or me henceforth you will have to ask us for it. That is how you will know that it is not an imposter. The safe word is *Jello.* If by any chance you at any point start to feel danger to you or anyone around you use the signaling word, *Rain*. These are magic words we have put a spell and jinxed as it works within the four walls here. Someone from our world will be here to help you in split seconds. All good? We may leave."

Mr. Raven angrily got up saying, "You mean we just sit around here and just wait." Clove responded, "That is the best that you can do for yourself and all. If you want to do something. Pray that this pain and suffering may pass and let the evil be defeated, so we may be victorious again," saying this she went and hugged them all. Father James gave her a wooden cross. Then Emerald and Clove apparated to his house.

In the drawing-room, seated on the sofa Clove spoke, "What is the plan?" Emerald said while he walked to the window, "We should go to the dungeons and check for clues, to know what is King Angus's next move. But before that, I need to meet with Queen Mother she needs to know you are here."

Emerald sent green sparks up in the sky from his window. After a while, a pigeon appeared with a parchment tied to its foot. That was from Queen Mother. It read as -

Dear Emerald,

I received your signal. I know that you are safe in your house. King Oberon has successfully united all Kingdoms. From the south, the water fairies with mermaids have come to our aid and will keep a watch. Fire fairies along with their dragons will keep guard on the east. The Sky fairies will guard the west. We are hoping the giants will help us in the North but we have not received their word. As you know they are not trustworthy. But we are working on it. As you read, a decision would be made. If they decline then the leprechauns should take over.

The Earth and the Forest Fairies have sided with King Angus, so he thinks he can defeat us.

King Angus has escaped along with Bossy and Tulip. I must warn you that Bossy is the one who aided in killing your father. He is quick in duels, his partner in crime. Tulip killed Camila; she is Bossy's companion. The trios have overthrown Addison, King Angus's son. As you read, he has taken charge of the kingdom. He has sent his son to the dungeon. He needs to be freed. His wife, Holly escaped in time and is under our protection.

Remember he is vicious and we have only one choice; to finish him. I urge you to free him and then only return to the palace.

Remember I love you. Be careful. He may not strike immediately. But we cannot either since the truce is made, we have to wait for him to attack. We need to find his weakness. I am sure you will find a way. Mab will be there soon to meet you. Do not leave till she is there.

Titania

Clove was the first to speak, "Good, so we have to go to the dungeon." Emerald burnt the parchment so that it would not fall into the wrong hands and be seen. He calmly replied to her saying, "Not we, only me." Clove smirked and said, "You can just not expect me to sit around and you have all the action. What about all the claims of safety?" Emerald looked at her with a stern face and said, "Very well, let's have some wine to quieten our nerves. I have not wished you a happy birthday yet. I trust this should be your first wine glass." Saying this he moved towards the table and poured out two glasses of wine. While she sat on the sofa. He secretly poured a decoction of Nux Moschata into her drink. With the right amount, she would comfortably sleep and not get in his way. He was guilty but as it is said 'all is fair in love and war'.

He walked towards Clove and handed over her glass "Happy Birthday! Clove. To health, wealth, and prosperity." By saying this Emerald clinked their glasses. She took her first sip. "Hmm! It tastes awful." Emerald smiled and said, "I guess it is better than the decoction I first gave you." Clove could not conceal her smile saying, "Way better." Emerald kept the conversation going and kept pouring wine. They spoke about how her birthday party was planned and all the guests. Her grocery store visit. She was happy and chirpy. Emerald was caught up observing her green eyes, her red hair flying in the cool breeze, and her smile, something about her was attracting him towards her. Was it the wine? These words were echoing in his mind, there was this sudden surge in him to kiss her that grew so strong as he moved in to close the gap. Queen Mab's entry was announced in the drawing room by a fairy. Both of them got up and curtsied to her. Emerald kissed her on her hand and greeted her and hugged her. Unlike Queen Mother, Clove found Princess Mab quite relaxed and laid back. Maybe as she lived her life alone and with a human, she could connect with her.

"Happy Birthday! Clove. Emerald get me a glass of wine. Will you?" saying this she sat on the sofa and asked Clove to sit too.

Chapter 22

Visit to the Dungeon

After the pleasantries were finished, Princess Mab laid the map of the dungeon in front of Emerald on the table. As Clove arose from the sofa, she felt dizzy and Emerald carried her to the adjacent bedroom. Clove was confused, drowsy, and sleepy. As he laid her down on the bed Emerald whispered into her ears saying, "Forgive me, Clove I spiked your drink, relax. You should wake up after five hours and I should be back by then." Emerald closed the door and walked towards his mother who was waiting for him and Clove drifted into a deep slumber.

"If I were you, I would use Passiflora decoction. Nevertheless, this way she is safe and she will be under my supervision." Princess Mab remarked. Emerald replied, "How did you know?" Princess Mab replied, "As I entered, I saw an empty vial near the wine bottle which you forgot to dispose of in a hurry, she had started sweating, and Oh! This is not the time for it." Emerald smiled and said, "You have the eyes of a hawk, Mother."

Princess Mab said, "I take that as a compliment. So, where was I? The dungeons as you see are a vast area that has a boundary wall made up of rocks. It has a huge iron gate with an eye welded in the center. Now each magical creature has access to its private dungeons. Roads are intersecting at right angles and blocks on either side. Each road is numbered, and the private dungeons have alphabetical numbering. Dungeons are entirely situated to the west of the waterfall. The entire area is guarded round the clock by goblins and they need to be paid in gold if we visit any prisoner inside. But solitary confinement cells cannot have visitors as their sins are grave and they need signatures of at least four kings. Mark my words even in our magical world, a king fears to sign, so we can rarely obtain it. Goblins are diminutive humanoid face creatures with broad foreheads, pointy noses and ears, long feet and fingers but the body is covered with hair and the resemblance is similar to a bat. These are mischievous and malicious they do not like magical creatures similar to them like leprechauns, gnomes, etc. Beware and never trust them. They have their hats soaked in human blood. So good, Clove is not accompanying you.

Our dungeons are to the north. Avenue Number 3, Block 16, and the prisoner in question will be Aida in cell number 4. King Oberon sent her there today this morning for twenty-four hours. So you have to go surrender your dagger and wand to the Goblin at the gate, as you enter, the second goblin will collect the gold coins, and a third goblin will accompany you to a podium where you write the name of the visitor you wish to meet on the blackboard with white chalk and if it is permissible, the goblin will pull the lever which will teleport you right in front of her cell, the patrolling goblin will be waiting to receive you. Aida has my wand in the hem of her dress. You cannot do magic there it's jinxed. But if you have to do it, would take them two minutes to get there. Aida will give you my wand, the patrolling goblin will take you to the solitary cell, and you will have to pay the goblin in gold there you will find the delirious Addison, who awaits you, and the goblin will take your leave. Are you with me son? "

"Why delirious?" asked Emerald. "Oh! Angus left him so. He manipulated his memory and left him there to rot." Replied Princess Mab

Saying this Mab paused to quench her thirst with wine. Emerald was looking closely at the map. While he was studying it, he realized that their cells were closer to solitary confinement. "It's fair as the solitary cells are close by."

"The solitary cells are guarded by a Griffin. Goblins do not prefer to be near it. Griffin has the head of an eagle covered with brown and white feathers and a pointy beak, has ears made of feathers, the wings are huge and they have the front legs of an eagle and body and hind legs including the tail of a lion. They cannot be defeated in the skies nor on land except by dragons. The swiftness of an eagle and the strength of a lion. "Mab was interrupted by Emerald who said, "Mother, are you scaring me or sacrificing me? What am I missing something here?"

Mab smiled and touched his face tenderly. "I love you son you need to know your enemy well." Saying this she continued, "You need to tie his feet first and then his chest. By doing so you are buying time for yourself to enter Addison's cell. Rumor has it, that Angus was placed in a different cell numbered J 49 all these years. He was shifted to Addison's cell A 14 on the ground floor a few days ago. Thereafter he disappeared in thin air."

Mab looked worried. She continued, "I assume there's something in that cell that can help you to apparate and you need to find it.'

Emerald enthusiastically said, "Oh! Dear me. The Griffin outside, the goblins around, and me in the cell. I hope my stay should not extend indefinitely." Princess

Mab was laughing, " If Angus came to me, I would tell him to keep you. He would return you the next day for sure. You are being over dramatic."

Emerald asked Princess Mab, "Mother, when do I leave?" Princess Mab replied, "Our goblin will stand on guard in an hour, so you can gather your things; we need our goblin in." Emerald had other plans in mind. He walked across the room to the adjacent bedroom where Clove was lying in the bed. She looked so beautiful and oblivious to the planning and scheming outside. Emerald had butterflies in his stomach. He did not know what caused it. Was it the dangers that lurked ahead of him or the attraction he was feeling for Clove? "Clove's family is just doing fine says Bigfoot. Only he is grumpy as they seem to have lost their appetite. What a shame! His culinary skills are put to no good. Oh! The puppy eyes! I know that look." Princess Mab was all excited like a child. "Keep it down, Mother!" Said Emerald. He carefully walked out without making a sound while Princess Mab followed around like a puppy waiting for a chance to tease him. "You like her don't you, you have my blessings!" Princess Mab was jumping with joy. "Mother, don't you have better things to do, please let me breathe, stop hovering around me. I have work to do," saying this Emerald walked himself to his room and shut the door in his mother's face. "Fine, I'll leave." Saying so she turned around. While Emerald was blushing to himself. He wanted to have a bath to cool his nerves and after that, he dressed himself and kept his blunt dagger and his old wand, took the gold coins in two velvety pouches, and hugged his mother promising her to meet again.

He apparated to the dungeons. The gate was huge and made of iron and an eye that was welded in, looked implicit. As he crossed it, a few steps ahead he saw rows of lockers on either side of the road as he walked further, he found five goblins seated on the chairs on either side of the road on the right side it read the entry and the left side showed the sign exit. Emerald reached for one of the goblins that sat free. The Goblin smirked, "Report yourself." Emerald replied, "Prince Emerald." Goblin continued, "Ah we have a prince, what you say to us means nothing. Your dagger and wand, please. Disclose if you have anything other than that which is magical." Emerald handed him his dagger, and wand and denied having anything else. The goblin wrapped it in a cloth and placed it in wooden lockers with a glass door he then gave Emerald a token and asked him to collect it on his way out. The locker then went underground and an empty locker appeared in its place. He was allowed to pass to the second checkpoint. At the second checkpoint on arriving there, he saw a huge building with a glass dome. As he entered, he saw forty counters where goblins were collecting gold and checking it from all magical creatures. "Token number 357 please proceed to counter number 40," said a hoarse male voice. That was Emerald's token and he walked to counter number 40 just to his right. The second goblin asked him. "Who do you wish to meet?" Emerald replied, "Aida, our fairy of the Kingdom of Sky." That second goblin wrote on a parchment and burnt it in fire. A book came flying from the shelves behind and was placed in front of the desk the goblin sat down, the book opened and the pages turned by itself, and Aida's page appeared. He addressed Emerald, "Petty thief. She stole the king's slippers. She sang all day and so we shifted her to another block three hours ago. She sang so well that we put her in front of the solitary cells to lift the mood of the prisoners. She is now in Avenue no 82, Block no 1 Cell No 5. Pay five gold coins." Emerald was shocked to hear this and turned pale. While paying the goblin the thought that worried him was that he was just in front of Addison's cell. The griffin would be difficult to take on as he would be easily exposed. The goblin counted each coin rubbed them on a stone pressed it between his teeth and then gave Emerald a parchment to walk towards the tents.

Emerald walked further. Everything was dark, cold, and poorly lit. There was a huge rubble of stones on either side of the road. He saw five tents heavily guarded. As he approached the tents he was stopped by one goblin. The third goblin asked, "Show me your parchment." The third goblin showed him to proceed to the tent number 3. Emerald walked towards it having cold feet. He was now not comfortable with this sudden change of the cell. He entered and, in the center, there was a glass case enclosing a blackboard having a lever outside the case. The fourth goblin asked him for the parchment and made him stand on a box marked with red and a pole where he would be strapped on top of the pole was a blackboard where the goblin wrote AIDA, AVENUE NO 82, BLOCK NO 1 CELL NO 5. He closed the glass case and the lever was pulled and Emerald went spiraling down. Upon reaching down the entire place was well lit with the help of a lamp post. The glass door was opened and he was set free of his restraints. The capsule was closed and it was sent up with a press of a red button. It was like a whole new city down there. There were buildings made of stone. It had stone walls on three sides and one side had iron bars. He could see carpets flying everywhere and all different magical creatures seated on different carpets headed towards their cells visiting their loved ones accompanied by two goblins. Emerald had a whole carpet to himself today as nobody beside him was visiting the Sky dungeons today at this hour. The goblin said, "Hold on tight as it is going to be a bumpy ride."

It was a bumpy ride as when the carpet rose from the ground Emerald was a little off balance so he caught on to the side, the cool breeze against his face made his hair fly as it made its way to its destination. Emerald curiously asked, "How are the prisoners transported?" To which the goblin replied, "We have three different gates. The west gate is the visitor's gate. The east gate is the prisoner's entrance while the south gate is the exit. The prisoners have a different protocol, I am not aware of much."

They had reached the cell it was on the ground floor. One goblin flew away with the carpet and the second one escorted him to the cell with a lamp. "You give my regards to Princess Mab; I tipped that fool to sing as my duty was changed this morning to this block. I must say she was good, it worked. Time for my reward." Saying so he stopped in front of Aida's cell. "First you take me to the solitary cells and then I pay you your reward." Saying so Emerald turned to Aida and said, "My mother's wand please." To which she apologetically replied," I am sorry it got lost during the cell transfer it must have fallen off." 'Ok, Emerald you can still do this. Improvise.' Emerald was saying this aloud to himself. No matter the reassurances his heart was beating faster.

He handed over the gold coins to the goblin and while he did so he heard a loud cry coming from the solitary cells after which he saw smoke rising in the distance. The goblin caught him and took him by the hand apparated in front of the solitary cells leaving him as planned.

Emerald could see a bleeding dragon lying down, a wounded fairy in front of Addison's cell, and the griffin dead on the other end. There were shattered glasses everywhere and huge raging fires and the freed prisoners apparating a total sight for chaos. He rushed to her and asked her if she was doing fine. To which she replied to take her to A14 cell. Emerald did as he was told, Addison had passed out due to the smoke. There was a fierce fight between the beasts that had caused so much destruction. She told him to press the cornerstone on the left wall and take the third right door out holding Addison. "Apparate while you can, tell Bossy, that I, Tulip loves him." Saying so Tulip left their world and rose petals were found where she lay. Emerald rushed towards Addison carried him and pressed the cornerstone.

Chapter 23

New Acquaintances

Emerald found himself in a room surrounded by mirrors. He scanned everywhere frantically for a door or a knob to be led out but to his surprise found none. In the meanwhile, Addison woke up saying, "Where am I? Who are you? Where are you taking me? Put me down." Emerald reassured him saying, "I am Prince Emerald. I wish to take you to your wife Queen Holly, she is in the protection of King Oberon, but all possible if I figure our way out." By then Emerald had put him down. "I think we should go to Grandpa, it will be safe there till I get my strength back," Addison said so and placed his hand on the mirror to the left by doing so a wooden door appeared and he opened the knob which led them both out into a dining room.

The dining room had stone walls. There was a window with olive green curtains drawn to the sides which let the sunlight in. A green-colored carpet was placed right in the middle of the dining room having a table, and comfortable seating for six people was placed. It had a chandelier in the center with twelve candles on it. Emerald helped Addison to be seated on the chair, drew the pitcher, and poured him a glass of water. "Pardon me, sir! Are you alright?" asked a housekeeper. Emerald's attention was drawn towards her. She looked concerned. "I should go fetch a doctor and inform the master." Saying so she hurried outside the room. "Addison! My dear God, are you alright?" saying so an aged gentleman with a fine dressing sense had rushed in. He had a well-kept French beard blue eyes with wrinkles and a wheat complexion. "Grandpa, the smoke, I am breathless, he helped me," said Addison passing out. "Let us take him to the adjacent room. I don't think we could escort him up." Addison's grandfather signaled Emerald to help him. Together they shouldered him to the adjacent room, placed him on the bed, and covered him. The doctor with a nurse was quick to arrive and asked them to leave the room. "I need to thank you for saving my grandson's life. We haven't been introduced formally. I was King Mabon, the ruler of the Earth Fairies, dethroned by now King Angus who is my son and Addison is my grandson. You would be?" asked Mabon. Emerald replied to him, "I am Prince Emerald, son of Princess Mab, Kingdom of the Sky." Mabon looked shocked, "I heard you were a leprechaun, good to know that your curse is broken. We all, I guess have been at the receiving end of unpleasant gifts, from my son King Angus, would not you agree?" Emerald just smiled, evading the question, "Do you live alone your majesty?"

Mabon's eyes showed only pain, his expression turned sad, "Son you have gone through a lot I understand, well I have too, I lost my wife, Violet, in childbirth. Angus was raised by his governesses, I was busy with the concerns of the kingdom, and I was not there for him. He never got love in his growing years so when he met your mother, I guess she was so beautiful, it was love at first sight and when she rejected him, he could not accept it too well that he lost her to a mundane. Ego, I tell you, can make one's heart too cold and it can shun away an ounce of good; be it deed or thought. After many years, although he was married to Diana, he was truly unhappy perhaps he wanted it this way. Princess Mab too didn't accept him even after all these years which only fueled the fire. What our world doesn't know is I had another son, Walter, he was an Eerie. One moment of my weakness. He lived with his mother as she chose to be away from this world." Mabon led Emerald upstairs into another room and opened the door to show a gentleman seated on a chair writing in a book placed on the desk who seemed to be engrossed in thought. It looked like a small study. All Emerald could see was his back. Mabon closed the door and continued to walk to another room leading the way, "What you do not know is I have kept him hidden from the world, all these years." They had reached the door to another room as King Mabon opened it, Emerald saw only pictures of Camila everywhere. She looked young and happy. On the head end, he saw a portrait of Camila and a man in each other's arms lost in love, ignorant of their surroundings looking at each other. King Mabon said, "My son Walter, is Clove's father." Emerald felt dizzy, he was at a loss of words he took a deep breath and sat on the bed. "He lost his mother, and since then I have kept him with me. Angus never visited me, but a few months ago when he did, he was upset to learn that Camila rejected Walter after learning about our family feud. Walter remained a bachelor. She gave her illegitimate child to care for to her friends as they were married and later went on to marry her friend Connor." "So, Angus killed her?" asked Emerald. Mabon continued, "Angus did go to meet her, and ask to leave Connor and live with Walter, on that fatal night, they got into a war with words and one thing led to another, Angus in a fit of anger asked Tulip to kill her and made it look like a suicide. Walter on learning this was deeply grieved and has lost his senses since then. He is consumed with grief and keeps writing her name day and night."

King Mabon drew a stool and sat in front of Emerald. "Son, I am old and I am tired. I want to end this blood bath that Angus has started; it was foolish of me to persuade

Tulip to set Addison free. Poor her; she left our world. I want you to help me, I want Addison to sit on the throne. I want Walter and his daughter reunited. I want Angus dead. Will you help me? Addison is freed and the news will reach him, he would want to take revenge. I will die both ways but this madness must stop."

"Master Addison is awake and doing fine. Would you like to meet him?" asked the housekeeper. "Yes, I would love to, please usher Prince Emerald to the guest room and serve him something to eat and drink whatever he may fancy." Saying so King Mabon rushed out of the room after taking Emerald's leave. The maid ushered Emerald to a room across the hallway. "What would you like to eat?" asked the housekeeper. "I don't have much of an appetite maybe something light." Replied Emerald.

King Mabon's truth had shaken Emerald, he did not know whether to trust it, but the offer was tempting he had to get the news delivered but how was the question? Would it be safe to send the message? Did he have a choice?

"Your Highness, I have brought back some coffee and vegetable sandwiches." the housekeeper laid the tray on the tables and drew a chair for him to sit on. Emerald sat in the chair. "Would you want anything else? May I leave?" asked the maid. "I want to send a letter to Queen Titania would you be able to do so?" asked Emerald. The housekeeper was quick to reply, "It can be arranged. I will bring you a parchment and quill." Saying so she left the room only to bring the things. Emerald quickly scribbled on the parchment and sealed it and gave it to her. She said, "I will ask Ronald to fly out with the dragon if you would be awaiting a reply." "I would love that as I am to await a reply." Said Emerald. She left at once to do the needful. Emerald munched on the snacks that lay before him. He slowly drifted off to sleep in the bed waiting for the reply eagerly.

It was late in the evening Emerald heard a knock at his door which woke him up. "Come in." He said with a sleepy voice. The housekeeper was back she had brought his reply with her. She spoke first, "Your Highness, the reply arrived soon after, but since you were asleep. I did not disturb you. You are asked to join King Mabon and his son Prince Walter for dinner in 45 minutes, he sent you a change of clothes in case you choose to freshen up. Shall I leave the reply on the table?" "No, I would like to read it first, thank King Mabon for the invite, I shall freshen up and change to join them soon." The housekeeper took his leave. Emerald quickly read the reply and was pleased with the outcome. He rushed to bathe and freshen up as dinner awaited him and so was his reply to the proposed question to King Mabon.

Chapter 24

Freed at Last

"There you are, I was beginning to worry, the clothes fit just fine, Addison would have his meal in the room, son, join us," King Mabon welcomed Emerald and showed him to his seat. King Mabon had already started on his meal with his son Walter. Emerald thanked them and served himself. "Have you given it a thought on what I said?" asked King Mabon. "As a matter of fact, yes I have," replied Emerald as he chewed over his meal. "How do we go about it? Do you have a plan, you will need my help?" King Mabon was accessing Emerald's response. They were interrupted by a housekeeper who rushed in saying, "Forgive me, your Majesty we are under attack the fairies from the Sky have seized this castle and we are outnumbered here. I need your orders." "Let them come in. Do not engage in a war." Said King Mabon.

"How are we doing?" said Princess Mab. Emerald arose to welcome his mother. "We were doing just fine till you came along." Grumbled King Mabon. "I did fine too till your son came along." Princess Mab replied. "Come to the point my lady. Spare us your grief." "King Oberon wants to annex the Kingdom of Earth and place the dethrone King Addison as his wife has taken asylum with us. You will be the proxy for Addison as King Oberon heard he is unwell. We have sent word to King Angus and he shall be here by nightfall and we will defeat him in a magical game of his choice to keep it fair and square, King Oberon wants less blood on his hands." Said Princess

Mab. "Very well, if I have to face him then be it so," said King Mabon. He continued eating signaled Princess Mab to her seat and said, "Be my guest. At least have a decent meal with us Mab."

Meanwhile, King Angus signals a housekeeper to let Bossy who had just returned meet King Oberon. "Your Majesty! I have bad news. King Oberon has captured King Mabon's castle, your son is sick and recovering but not in a position to be shifted, and your stepbrother is the same, still in shock. They have placed King Mabon as your opponent in a magical game that you will play instead of war. They want minimum blood loss. Your Majesty let me know, your servant is listening."

"I heard about Tulip. I am sorry. Bossy, you served me well. This is the time I have to face my loved ones and my enemies. Do not worry for I am confident, victory is mine whatever the outcome. Bossy, I release you from my service. Serve my son well. Go in peace." said King Angus. "Your majesty, are you sacrificing yourself?" "Oh! Bossy time has come where I have to give answers and get answers. I will not back out. It has been a while since I played with my father. Now go, I need to rest." "Your majesty forgives me but what game will you choose?" "I thought about the enchanted snakes and ladder, the fairy's trial," replied King Angus. "Then you will need my help. I cannot desert you now after knowing this." Bossy, was pleading, trying to put sense into him. "Very well, meet me at nightfall, together we will enter the lion's den. Send the parchment with William so they prepare for it with the forest fairies."

King Mabon had a visitor, it was King Alfred, of the Kingdom of Fire. He was received by King Mabon, Princess Mab, and Prince Emerald. After pleasantries were exchanged King Alfred was the first to speak, "I received word that King Angus wishes to play. 'The Enchanted Snakes and Ladder, the Fairy's Trial'. Well, are you not too old for it? I was worried for you. I will prepare for it though; you must know it has to be fair."

Legend whispered of a time when chaos threatened to engulf the forest, and only those deemed worthy by the game could safeguard its magic. Thus, the enchanted Snakes and Ladders became a rite of passage, a test of character for those who sought to protect the realm. This game is not for the faint-hearted which occurs in the enchanted forest, where magic dances on every leaf and whispers through every breeze. This game was crafted by the ancient fairies themselves. But this wasn't just any game; it was a trial, a test of wit, courage, and luck. For in this version of the game, one didn't just aim to reach the end; they aimed to survive. The snakes were not mere pitfalls but guardians, and the ladders, pathways to salvation. Each encounter was a gamble, with victory as the prize and defeat as the consequence.

The rules were simple yet perilous: players would traverse the enchanted board, facing challenges and obstacles at every turn. Some squares held friendly creatures offering aid, while others hid cunning serpents ready to strike. But the true test lay in the final stretch – a treacherous climb where only the bravest dared to tread.

And so, with every roll of the dice and every step forward, players ventured into the unknown, their fates intertwined with the whims of destiny. Some fell to the serpents' venomous bite, their dreams shattered amidst the tangled vines. Yet, for the resilient few who emerged victorious, glory awaited – not just as champions but as guardians of the enchanted forest, sworn to protect its magic for generations to come.

As seasons turned and years passed, the enchanted Snakes and Ladders became a legend whispered among the trees, a story of courage and perseverance passed down through generations. Though the game itself faded into memory, its legacy endured; a reminder of the power of unity, resilience, and the magic that dwelled within everyone.

"Of course, these bones can still take on silly games," said King Mabon. "I heard Bossy would be his guide. Have you chosen yours?" asked King Alfred. "Oh! Please he is a chicken, he backed out when he heard about it. My son, Prince Emerald will play and I will be his guide." "You know Mab it's Prince Angus we are talking about. He will go to any extent to win this." Said, King Alfred. "I know we are prepared. I have to settle old scores with him." Said Princess Mab. King Alfred took their leave to make the necessary arrangements.

The time was quick to fly, it was nightfall. As promised King Angus and Bossy had reached the enchanted forests after Princess Mab, Emerald, King Mabon, and Clove had arrived. King Alfred explained the rules. King Angus and Emerald decided to traverse the forests and Princess Mab and Bossy would serve as guides to the enchantments in the play. Clove was there as she had awakened and heard everything, she wanted to meet Emerald and so had spent time with him after King Alfred had left. She was teary-eyed but Emerald had promised her of his return and she was not ready to lose another dear one.

"Can you please stand at the starting line." requested King Alfred. The entire forest kingdom had turned up for the game as it was a while since they had one. King Alfred stuck the ground with his wand, the ground divided, and the snakes and ladder game appeared on the ground it was oval, and in the center was the finish square. The snakes kept on changing, the ladders shifted too. The crowd roared and cheered seeing the board appear. They too, were seated around the board on the stands. King Alfred placed his wand on Emerald and he transfigured into a Leprechaun playpiece while King Angus turned into a king riding a horse playpiece. After they turned into play pieces King Alfred flicked his wand and they could view the enchanted forests and their players live in the sky. Princess Mab and Bossy were given their dice each. King Alfred asked Princess Mab to roll the dice. She was happy to see a six. She rolled dice and it stopped on number three, the Leprechaun play piece moved three places on the board while in the enchanted forest, Emerald was spoken by the spirits to take three long strides ahead. That's how he knew Princess Mab had rolled a six and had got three on the next roll. It was Bossy's turn and he rolled a 4, followed by a 5, and then landed on a 6. He was relieved to see the six. The next dice he rolled was number 6. King Alfred came forward with his choices. "Do you wish to roll the dice or try your luck at an enchantment?" Asked King Alfred. "I choose an Enchantment," Bossy said so he was quick to choose. "Very well pick from the enclosed wooden box case, only one can you choose." Saying so King Alfred ushered him towards the box. Bossy picked a hidden path. Angus was directed six strides ahead and to the right, Emerald raised his eyebrows watching him cross, while on the board King Angus's playpiece moved six places and a cave appeared.

    Angus kept on walking and he found a den, the den was covered by vines and Angus knew he had to enter it and this was a challenge that Bossy had chosen for him. As he entered the den, he heard his wife's voice calling out, "Angus it's me, Diana. Welcome to my den." Saying so a unicorn appeared in front of him. The unicorn was purest white and had a horn that was gleaming brightly. The unicorn its eyes sparkled with a gentle gaze, filling the place with a sense of peace and tranquility. "Is that you?" asked King Angus. "Angus, ask what lies before you and not what lies in the past. This den where you're standing is the first enchantment, if you pass the test, you will be given the Healing Elixir: a vial of sparkling liquid drawn from the purest springs of the enchanted forest. This elixir possesses potent healing properties, capable of restoring vitality and warding off the effects of injury or affliction. A Guidance Amulet: a shimmering amulet adorned with a radiant crystal at its center. This amulet acts as a guiding light in the darkest of times, illuminating hidden paths and revealing truths that are obscured from anyone's eyes." "What is it that you demand of me?" "Find where they are placed the faster you do the higher you go in the game." As Angus entered, he saw a waterfall, and right on top were two vials emitting light radiantly. He knew he had to climb the waterfall but the stones were covered with moss and the stones were sharp and slippery from the moisture, the air, and the erosion from the water. He tried using the wand but magic didn't work. He had to think out of the box. It was a race against time.

Princess Mab had rolled the dice and Emerald had landed on the snake. He was bitten by it and was wounded, after a while, he had a ladder and climbed slowly, her heart was bleeding knowing he was bleeding. She was unlucky as she had not gotten a six, thus enchantments weren't given, he was injured but kept progressing slowly. He climbed to the number 35 on the board.

"I know I can't use magic, I can't climb it either I have failed trying to do so, and I need your help. I am exhausted", implored King Angus. "Angus ask me the correct question" was the unicorn's reply. Angus thought for a while. "Will you fly me to the vial?" asked Angus. "Yes! Hop on," was her reply. Angus alighted her, she flew him over and gave the vials to him. When he held on to the vials, he found himself in the area marked 40. As he turned around, he saw an injured Emerald behind him.

"It's a six finally!" yelled Princess Mab. She hurried to the enchantments and brought out alliances. That means Emerald would choose a spirit from the enchanted forest or someone from his world. Emerald was bleeding profusely after the bite; the spirits asked his preference for which he whispered Clove's name. King Alfred summoned her and pointed his wand towards her and she appeared as a queen playpiece and climbed to his square and lay aside him on the board. But She was physically teleported to Emerald as she entered the game. "Clove, I just can't go alone the poison is weakening." Emerald, was mumbling. "I am here now we can do it! I want you to be alert for me and I will be your strength." By saying so, she had placed his hand over her shoulder and tied the injured leg with the nearest vine to her so they could pace faster, "You know he is ahead." Said Emerald. "We have to play this honestly. No matter what happens."

Both were climbing the places as Emerald and Angus were giving each other a tough fight even destiny this time sided with no one as luck played a very big role. Bossy cried out aloud, "Six it is." King Alfred signaled Bossy to move towards the enchantments. This time it was a cursed dice. The Cursed dice are enchanted objects imbued with unpredictable magical properties. When rolled, they can produce a wide range of effects that may either aid or hinder the player's progress through the game. However, the nature of these effects is entirely random, making cursed dice a double-edged sword that can tip the balance of fortune in unexpected ways. It was Bossy's turn and as he rolled the cursed dice; 'Echoes of the Past' appeared over the dice. King Angus disappeared from the enchanted forest only to find himself in his mother's arms. It was that fatal day when he was born and would lose his mother. To be embraced in his mother's arms was a great solace, her smell her touch everything was so enchanting. Her face, although she was exhausted looked so radiant and her smile refreshing. She was kissing his face and she held on to him she saw the amulet, and she summoned his governess. "This is my amulet I presented it to Princess Diana, on her birth to betrothed her to the heir of our kingdom how did it land in my son's hand?" "Forgive me your Highness I know nothing of it," said the governess. "If it's on my son's hand means he has time travelled here for a purpose," said his mother. Just then a fairy entered her chamber. "Your majesty, King Mabon has been informed about the birth. He congratulates you and sends this ring for you and a chain for the prince. He will join you after some time as the mundane delivered a son before you and they will be arriving soon." Said the fairy. "I don't know what crime I have done to lose favor in his sight, he chose a mundane over me, I curse him, may they be separated and I receive the share of my love much due to me." Saying so she sadly looked at the governess. The fairy again rushed in informing, "Your Majesty, King Mabon has arrived, he looks happy for the Mundane has arrived here with her son." Saying so she left her. "Oh! Now he has brought her too and his bastard eerie child." Saying this she asked his governess to place Angus in the cradle. "Violet! Oh! There you are. How are you? Where is my son?" asked King Mabon and he walked to the cradle to have a glimpse of his prince. "To what do I owe your grace's visit?" asked Violet. "I know I haven't been around, Violet you knew our marriage was out of compromise. But I now have found love and I desire to live with happiness. You will have my respect but my heart lies with her. Forgive me." said King Mabon. "Very well then leave us." Said Violet in anger, she could not tolerate him. King Mabon left her and she fainted. She was bleeding profusely, in pain and soon she succumbed to the bleed and left the world with violets on the bed. King Angus is brought back to the enchanted forest and finds his amulet missing. The enchantments asked him to move forward. And so, he obliges.

Emerald was on 94 after being bitten by three more snakes but he never gave up alongside Clove and he continued, while King Angus was on 91. The victory was near and again it was Bossy's turn to roll the dice and it turned out to be a six. It seemed like Angus had luck. This time Bossy rolled out deception for Prince Emerald. Princess Mab was nervous she didn't know what the outcome would be. King Mabon was asked to choose sides, he was willing to betray Prince Emerald over his son King Angus as it is said 'blood is thicker than water.' Princess Mab was in tears, cursing she said, "You vermin, you will rot in hell." King Mabon mocking bowed before her and smirked.

King Alfred sent him in the game and the crowd cheered on. All the three in the enchanted forest heard a spirit who greeted them with a melodic whisper that stirred the very essence of their souls. They felt drawn to it however, King Angus warns Clove and Emerald not to partake in it as this could be an enchantment or a deception that would test their luck and gain the favor of the Guardian. But Clove and Emerald eagerly accepted the offer, unaware of the treachery that lay ahead. Clove rolls the dice on the request of the spirits and they see King Mabon calling them in their direction towards the finish, Emerald not aware of the deception is unfortunately bitten by a hidden snake at 97 proceeding towards King Mabon and now are relocated and land on no 18 for the price for choosing deception. Seeing his father there deceiving another soul, King Angus cannot control himself and he walks towards his father leaving his victory behind, and stabs him in his back with his dagger. A shocked King Mabon looks on to see that he has been stabbed by his son.

"My son why did you betray me?" asked Mabon in his dying state. "This is for the death of my mother, this is for the neglect in my growing years, this is for deceiving them when they needed you the most. You were, are, and will be selfish always." Angus was overcome by his rage, he had lost the sense of right and wrong. Seeing the death of King Mabon the spirits of the forests are unhappy and the snakes leave their places and move toward King Angus, the snakes overpower him as he fights to kill a few, the numbers get overwhelming and he is left with no choice but to surrender as he is sucked in the forest he looks in the direction of Clove and Emerald pleading for a peaceful death with his eyes rather than facing the wrath of the spirits. Emerald turns towards Clove and together they raise their hands and point their wands and unanimously yell the killing curse "Kifo!"

Before he is struck by the death curse he throws the Healing Elixir vial in Clove's direction, not only does she catch it but also empties the contents into Emerald's mouth to find his wounds to heal. The pathway opens up and they climb up ladders to reach the center as their opponent is drawn away from the game, when they reach the end of the game the forest fairies as a token of their victory ask them each a chance to claim their reward.

Clove decides to speak to the soul of her mother. Her wish is granted the spirits call her mother to appear before her. Clove is all teary-eyed seeing her mother. Camilla is the first to speak, "My baby, you have made me proud today, I cannot believe the sportsman spirit and the courage you displayed here. You were his strength and you didn't let your friend down despite the risk. I love you, sweetie." Clove was at a loss for words. Finally, she meekly responds, "Mom I love you and miss you. I want to hug you one last time. If only I knew you were my mother I would have changed a lot of things" "No don't blame yourself. I know you were in the best of hands. I needed you to be safe and away from the spotlight. So, Angus wouldn't harm you. Since he is no more can you do me a favor, I want you to meet Walter, your biological father we couldn't be together as the magical world would tear us apart but I know he needs you more than anyone now. Be the closer he needs and always know I love you and tell Walter that I loved him too till my last breath. Tell Connor and Chloe that I am happy for them. Connor was kind to marry me and be the support I needed." Camila slowly faded away.

The spirits asked Emerald for his reward. He chooses, to meet his father's soul. Jack Murray appears before him. Emerald looks at him and speaks up, "Dad, I am the unfortunate son, who could never meet you. I wanted to see you and listen to your voice." Jack smiles, "Son, I am proud of you, you have my blessings, and I know when your time comes you will rule wisely. I loved your mom and I love you too, too bad we could never meet. But take care of Clove, she has been through a lot and you and Mab have too. I know the best is yet to come for you all. I will always be with you, whenever you miss me close your eyes and you will hear a voice in your head. That will be me." Jack disappears and Clove and Emerald cross the finish line.

King Alfred teleports them back in his presence from the game, an overjoyed Princess Mab runs over to hug them both. The crowds cheer and applaud their victory.

Bossy dejected leaves to report to his new master King Addison and he is stopped by Emerald. "There is something I want you to know, Tulip was very brave, she was beautiful, and she told me to tell you that she loved you. I am sorry mate that you lost her. After I met my dad today I forgive you. I wish you all the very best." Bossy replied, "Well, I knew she loved me, I just didn't know the end was so near, I am sorry, I was following orders there was nothing personal with your dad. My friend there you have some mate (pointing in the direction of Clove), don't lose her." They both hugged each other to part ways and never to cross paths again.

Chapter 25

Love Conquers

Emerald, Princess Mab, and Clove apparate to King Mabon's palace. Clove's emotions are running a roller coaster ride inside her. She would be meeting her father for the first time. She wasn't prepared to face rejection. She had lost Charles and Connor was more of a friend than a father figure. She was yearning for a fatherly figure and this was the opportunity and she had to cease it.

Emerald wanted to give her the privacy they needed. Emerald apparated to the kingdom of Sky to meet his uncle and aunt. While Mab sat to write a parchment to Clove's family in the Oak tree waiting for news about Clove. The maid leads her to Walter's room. As she entered the room, Walter ceased his writing. Clove signaled the housekeeper to leave them and she approached him quietly. "Who is it?" asked Walter. Clove stood there quietly waiting for him to turn. Not getting a reply made angry Walter turned to find Clove standing in front of him.

"You resemble an acquaintance so dear to me. What is your name? Who do you wish to see?" Asked Walter. "I am Clove Campbell Burns. Your daughter. Born to Camila." Replied Clove. On hearing her response Walter arose from his chair and ran and hugged her. He did not utter a single word, both were crying out loud, was it because they had found each other, or was it they both missed Camilla, or the pain of separation none could guess. The silence did the talking for both and that brought upon the closure of the pain that Clove and Walter so very much needed.

"Bravo son, you did it." King Oberon had leaped with joy from his throne only to hug Emerald. He was proud that Emerald was victorious and King Angus was out of their lives like a bad dream, they had lost much but now they had amassed the Kingdom of Earth. King Oberon was happy that he had made the right choice for the throne.

"Connor! Come here quickly, Everyone Bignose just got this parchment delivered, and Clove and Emerald are safe. King Angus was defeated and dead left to his fate. Clove meets her biological dad, Walter, and Angus's stepbrother as we speak." Chloe was excited to release the tension that was built over the two days. That meant they could now step foot in their house. Everybody was hugging, there were tears and Thanksgiving prayers were said. They all decided to pack their things. Conner and Chloe decided to stay back a few days at the house. "Connor do you think that our daughter could be in love." Asked Chloe. "What brings upon this hypothesis?" Asked Connor in return. "It just occurred to me Clove was willing to take part in, despite the danger." "There could be another motive?" Reassured Connor. But something Chloe felt so deeply that she couldn't explain. It could be her gut feeling or intuition she couldn't say for now.

"Hail! King Addison, Hail! Queen Holly" The fairies of the Sky and Earth were overjoyed to see King Addison and Queen Holly back on the throne as today was their coronation.

But two souls who weren't happy, rather fighting they were Emerald and Clove. Clove was in tears begging him to reconsider her proposal. "I love you, Emerald, are you blind? Can't you see my affection for you? I do not care if our union needs sacrifices, I am willing to make them. They are mine and not yours to choose." "Have you not learned from what our families have been through? You still dive deeper for more trouble. Clove, I do not love you. I want a fairy as my mate and not a human is that clear, that settles it." Emerald lays the golden ring on Clove's finger, one that she had thrown towards him to bind him to her. "Now onwards I am not bound to you anymore." she gave him her handkerchief and set him free. A choice both made against their will.

Emerald with a heavy heart places a magical charm on her and puts her to sleep in her house in the city so that she forgets him. He meets her family and thanks them all for trusting her. "I love her and she loves me, but we are of different worlds, she will have to choose one and forfeit the other, I cannot see her lose the family who she loves dearly, sometimes sacrificing one's love can bring a greater good." Emerald was in tears with Clove's mother. "Isn't that her choice, not yours," remarked Chloe. Connor endorsed his views, and together they decided to erase everyone's memories of Emerald and their world.

Clove wakes up to be seated in the dining room with Connor on her left and Chloe on her right, Father James in front, Mr. Walter seated next to him, and Grandpa and Grandma on either end. It's been a week since her eighteenth birthday and she will be heading to medical school, she is all excited. Her birthday party was great and she met her biological dad who turned up searching for her at it. It had taken a lot of courage for him to realize his mistake and to own up to find her and together they were putting the pieces of their life together cherishing Camila's memories.

Chloe and Connor were excited about Clove's achievement. Clove was hoping to find love for she hadn't anyone in her life so far, at least. Walter would be her local guardian so they could spend some time together and get to know each other.

Emerald ruled the kingdom of Sky for King Oberon. The memories with Clove were sufficient for him to be happy. If, the love was real Emerald believed that he would see her again maybe not in weeks, months, or years, but at some point, they would connect and next time they would do it right but for now they would be two strangers. It only meant that he gave her life and peace back. He wanted her to live her life the way she deserved it. Meeting her and falling in love wasn't a mistake after all. It was God's way of giving them a lesson so that they would carry on for the rest of their lives. Even if their story ended here. He would never forget her chapter as that would be his favorite part of his book. Despite the temporary nature of their story.

Sometimes all love stories need not have happy endings. But the happiness you get knowing that the person you love is happy and safe means the world to you. Emerald loved Clove but he knew their worlds were apart, love should always be selfless, pure, kind, and giving as his. It only makes one stronger and such, I tell you are rare diamond to find if you do cling on to it.

The End